SECRETS OF
CASTILLO DEL ARCO

TRISH MOREY

~ Bound by his Ring ~

HARLEQUIN®

entertain, enrich, inspire™

Recycling programs for this product may not exist in your area.

ISBN-13: 978-0-373-52897-4

SECRETS OF CASTILLO DEL ARCO

FIRST NORTH AMERICAN PUBLICATION 2013

Copyright © 2012 by Trish Morey

TRISH MOREY wrote her first book at age eleven for a children's book-week competition. Entitled *Island Dreamer*, it told the story of an orphaned girl and her life on a small island at the mouth of south Australia's Murray River. *Island Dreamer* also proved to be her first rejection—her entry was disqualified. Shattered and broken, she turned to a life where she could combine her love of fiction with her need for creativity—Trish became a chartered accountant! Life wasn't all dull, though, as she embarked on a skydiving course, completing three jumps before deciding that she'd given her fear of heights a run for its money.

Meanwhile, she fell in love and married a handsome guy who cut computer code and Trish penned her second book—the totally riveting, *A Guide to Departmental Budgeting*—while working for the N.Z. Treasury.

Back home in Australia, after the birth of their second daughter, Trish spied an article saying that Harlequin® was actively seeking new authors. It was one of those eureka moments—Trish was going to be one of those authors!

Eleven years after reading that fateful article (actually June 18, 2003, at 6:32 p.m!), the magical phone call came and Trish finally realized her dream.

According to Trish, writing and selling a book is a major life achievement that ranks right up there with jumping out of an airplane and motherhood. All three take commitment, determination and sheer guts, but the effort is so very, very worthwhile.

Trish now lives with her husband and four young daughters in a special part of south Australia, surrounded by orchards and bushland and visited by the occasional koala and kangaroo.

You can visit Trish at her website, www.trishmorey.com, or drop her a line at trish@trishmorey.com.

Other titles by Trish Morey available in ebook:

Harlequin Presents®

3093—THE SHEIKH'S LAST GAMBLE *(Desert Brothers)*
3087—DUTY AND THE BEAST *(Desert Brothers)*
3045—FIANCÉE FOR ONE NIGHT

With grateful thanks to Ellen, Charlie and Claire for being my captive carpool brainstormers. Thank you so much for your interest and your input and energy and most of all, thank you for Venice. You guys rock!

And with thanks, as ever, to my fabulous Maytoners, for Coogee Beach and fish and chips, for making me laugh and cry and commiserate and celebrate, but with thanks, most of all, for once again making magic happen in the shape of words.

For it must be a kind of magic.

Thank you!

Trish

xxx

PROLOGUE

Paris

'Promise me something, Raoul. Grant a dying man one last wish.'

The old man's voice was thready and thin, little more than a whistle on his breath and no contest for the battery of machines beeping their presence around the bed. Raoul leaned closer. 'You mustn't talk that way, Umberto.' Raoul placed his hand over the old man's, trying not to damage the papery skin or nudge the needle projecting from the back of his claw-like hand; trying to pretend it was nowhere near as bad as it was. 'You are as strong as an ox,' he lied, wishing it were true. 'The doctor said—'

'The doctor is a fool!' the old man interjected, dissolving into a fit of coughing that left him wheezing in its wake. 'I am not afraid of death. I know my time has come.'

Wiry fingers clumsily overturned those of his visitor's, squeezing down as if to emphasise the urgency of his words, even though his once-legendary strength was gone, his fingers grown weak. 'But I fear what might happen once I am gone. Which is why I summoned you. You must promise me now, Raoul, before it is too late...'

The old man sagged against the pillows, his eyes closed in an ashen, sunken face, his sudden outburst taking its toll. For the first time Raoul was struck with the realisation that there would be no coming back: this time his oldest friend, his mentor—and the closest thing to family he had known for more than a decade—was dying. He had to force himself to stay and not flee from the room and the heavy knot tightening in his gut.

'You know I would do anything for you, Umberto,' he uttered in a voice that felt like gravel in his throat. 'You have my word. Ask, and it shall be.'

An eternity passed, an eternity filled with beeping machines that were the only sign Raoul had that his old friend had not already passed, until with a sigh his eyes fluttered open, watery and dim, his voice tinged with affection. 'Look after Gabriella for me. When I die, she will be vulnerable. I will not rest unless she is safe.'

He touched his free hand to the old man's shoulder to reassure him, his fingers encountering little more than bone. 'Then rest easy, old friend. Nothing will happen to her. I would be honoured to act as her guardian.'

The old man surprised him, snorting a protest instead of uttering the thanks he'd half-anticipated. Raoul was halfway to celebrating this spark of life, a glimpse of the Umberto that once was, until the words his old friend had said in response registered in his mind—impossible words, words that made the blood roar in his ears, sending thoughts of celebration tumbling and smashing like debris caught up in the first destructive wave of a tsunami.

He stood, unable to sit while the roar of the wave churned through him, and turned away from the bed, raking a damp hand through his hair and tugging at his tie, looking ceiling-ward for the air-conditioning vents. God, but it was hot in here.

'Raoul, did you hear me?' The thread of Umberto's frail words came on a thin wire that dug its way into him, slowing his retreat.

'I heard you,' he said—*every last word*—but that didn't stop Umberto from repeating them now, driving that sharp wire deeper and deeper into his psyche where it twisted and grew poisoned barbs.

'You must marry her, Raoul! Promise me you will marry Gabriella.'

Madness! He dragged in air tainted with the smell of impending death, disinfectant and the chemical sprays designed to disguise them all yet failing miserably, and threw his head back, hating what was happening— hating even more what he was hearing. Wasn't it bad enough that his old friend was dying? It had to be some kind of madness, he decided, for his friend to propose such insanity. 'You know that is not possible. Besides,' he added, remembering the last time he'd seen the girl, 'Even if I was crazy enough to marry again, surely Gabriella is too young?'

'A woman now.' Umberto blinked away tears, his voice breaking with emotion. 'Twenty-four years of age.'

Raoul was shocked by the invisible slide of time; cursed the years he had lost in the mire of another age.

Had it really been that long? Then again, maybe this made it better, easier. 'Then surely she is old enough to choose her own husband?'

'And if she chooses Consuelo Garbas?'

'Manuel's brother?' Raoul lifted disbelieving hands to his temples, driving fingertips deep into the veins that pounded like drums. God, but could this nightmare get any worse?

The name Garbas was seared on his soul, the letters burned deep, so deep that his bones ached at its mention. It was a name he'd hoped he'd heard for the last time a long, bleak time ago.

Yet he should have known that ridding himself of this curse would never be that easy. The Garbas family was like a black hole, sucking life from the world around, devouring anyone and anything in its path. He turned back, moved closer to the bed, needing to know despite himself. 'What does he want with Gabriella?'

'He's been sniffing around her like a hyena waiting for a carcass, waiting for her to turn twenty-five when she can claim her inheritance.' The old man paused, catching his breath, although the rise and fall of the covers over his chest was barely discernible. 'He knows I would never permit her to marry him. So now he waits for me to die before he makes his move.'

Raoul nodded. 'Hyena' was right. It was the way his kind operated: scavengers; scum, the lot of them. Only their massive wealth gave them entree into high society, lending them a veneer of respectability so brittle it was a wonder it didn't shatter every time they drew breath.

And now one of them was after Gabriella? 'She doesn't know?'

Umberto scoffed. 'He would hardly tell her the truth. She knows only that his brother died in tragic circumstances. She thinks that gives them something in common.' The old man sighed and gave a hint of a wistful smile as he shook his head. 'I have tried to warn her but Gabriella sees only the good in everyone—even the likes of him. And all the time he plays her like a fish on a line, knowing he has the advantage of time. So, you see, I have no one to turn to but you. You must marry her, Raoul,' he said, lifting his head shakily from the pillow in a supreme effort that saw the cords in his neck stand out tight, his watery eyes turn glassy in their intensity. '*You* must keep her safe. You must!'

He collapsed back into the pillows to catch his breath, the rapid beep of machines filling the void, while Raoul sat down by his side and bowed his head, his thoughts in turmoil, conflicted beyond measure.

Damned if he would let a Garbas worm his way into Umberto's granddaughter's fortune. Damned if he would ever let that happen after what he had suffered. But Raoul was the last person who could keep her safe.

Besides, did Umberto really think it would be such a simple matter to get a twenty four year old woman—any woman, for that matter—to agree to marry him? Why should she give him a second glance when he could give her nothing in return? She would be some kind of fool if she did.

He took his friend's hand again, half-wondering, half-knowing that this would be the last time they met.

'Umberto, old friend—*my friend*—I love you with my life, but this makes no sense. There must be a better way to keep Gabriella safe and I will find it. But I would be no kind of husband for your granddaughter.'

'I'm not asking you to love her!' he blustered from the bed, the machines beside him going into overdrive. 'Just marry her. Keep her safe!' The door burst open, a nurse rushing through, pushing the visitor aside as she checked her patient.

'Visit's over,' she snapped out without looking over her shoulder. 'You're upsetting my patient.'

Raoul raised his face to the ceiling in supplication and frustration. When he looked back at the bed where the nurse fussed, checked and adjusted drips and machines, his old friend looked so forlorn and desperate and beyond tired, a shadow of a man who had once been great. It struck Raoul that his last moments, his last days, should not be wasted in worry such as this, even if it meant promising the impossible so that he might at least die in peace. Umberto deserved that at least.

'I'll marry her, old friend, if that is what you ask,' he said, ignoring the warning scowl he earned in reward from the nurse, grinding the words out between his teeth as the wire in his gut pulled inexorably tighter and trying desperately not to think of the cost to them both. 'I'll marry her.'

CHAPTER ONE

Three weeks later

WINTER had come early, the late-September day dressed in drab colours as if the planet itself was mourning the death of her grandfather. But the inclement weather found only empathy with Gabriella D'Arenberg, the damp air and misty rain matching her mood as she stood beside her grandfather's flower-strewn grave in the Cimetiere de Passy. Then the last of the mourners whispered condolences and pressed cold lips briefly to her cheeks before drifting away along the path.

She would leave shortly too, once Consuelo had returned from the call he had excused himself to take, and they would join everyone at the hotel where the caterers were no doubt already serving canapés and cognac. But for now Gabriella was happy to be left alone in quiet reflection in the cold, dank stillness of the graveyard. Here, under the shadow of the Eiffel Tower, there was nothing to intrude, the sounds of the city barely penetrating the stone walls.

Until a dark shadow made her gasp and look around.

He appeared out of the fog, tall, broad and dark as

night as he moved stealthily between the funeral sculptures, the winged angels and fat cherubs suspended ghost-like in the swirling mist as he passed. A shiver of recognition—or was it of relief?—washed through her and bizarrely, for the first time that day, she felt warm.

Raoul.

She had seen him at the service; it had been impossible to miss his dark presence in the back of the tiny crowded chapel. Her heart had lifted at the prospect of seeing him again after so many years, only to exit the chapel to a bubble of disappointment when she had found him nowhere amongst the mourners gathered outside.

Raoul, who with his intense black eyes and passionate mouth had been her every adolescent fantasy—dark fantasies she'd had no right to imagine. Wicked fantasies that brought a blush to her cheeks just thinking about them. And, when she'd got news that he'd married, she'd cried for two days solid. She'd cried for him a year later when she'd learned of his wife's death. Thank God he had no idea about any of it or she could never face him now. Thank God she was over all that.

The crunch of boots on gravel grew louder, his long leather coat swirling about his legs, his hair pulled back into a ponytail that served to accentuate the strong lines and angles of his chiselled features. His eyes, if anything, were even more intense than she remembered under that dark slash of brow. Tortured, even. And something about that intensity frightened her a little, just as if his purposeful stride held a portent of danger, sending a tremor skittering down her spine.

The mist, she thought in explanation, as she continued to log his approach with her eyes. The cold, swirling air...

The air shifted and parted before him and then he was there, standing before her, a mountain of blackness in a mist-shrouded world, so tall that she had to tilt her head back to look up at him and his unflinching expression. He didn't smile. She didn't expect him to, not really, not this day.

But this was Raoul, an old family friend, so she dismissed her feelings of foreboding and danger and ventured a nervous smile of greeting, slipping her hands instinctively into his as easily as she had once done, relishing their instant warmth, thinking, *you came.* 'Raoul, it's so good to see you.'

For a moment he seemed to tense, and she wondered if she'd overstepped the mark by presuming familiarity. Then his hands squeezed hers and the tightness around his mouth relaxed just enough to give an answering smile that still spoke of sadness and loss. 'Gabriella,' he said in a way that seemed to cherish every syllable as he uttered it.

Then he leaned down to kiss first one cheek, and then the other, slow, lingering kisses. She shuddered under the brush of his lips against her flesh, his warm breath curling into hers and peeling back the years. She breathed him in, taken by the way he smelt so familiar, of clean skin and warm leather and the same woody notes of his signature scent that she recalled—yet there was so much more besides, as if what she'd remembered had been but a shadow of his essence.

'I am so sorry for your loss.' He drew back then, letting her hands drop, and she tried desperately not to be disappointed by his absence, shoving her hands in her coat pockets, not just to keep them warm but more to stop them reaching out for him. Those teenage fantasies might have been behind her, but Raoul was here now, real, broad and achingly close. Inside her pockets, her hands curled into fists.

'I didn't know you were coming,' she managed a little shakily, surprised he could still affect her so deeply and so fundamentally, even after so many years. 'Or you could have stayed at the house. Where are you staying? You should have let me know.'

He rattled off the name of a hotel that barely registered in the force of the impact of seeing him again. But then, she was hardly herself right now. Memories, especially memories of anything and anyone connected to her grandfather, seemed all too willing to bubble to the surface. Raoul had been close to her grandfather for longer than she had, their two families intertwined as long as she could remember, at least until the tragedy that had wiped out both sets of parents. 'And of course,' she said, acknowledging that truth, 'It's your loss too.'

'Umberto was a good man,' he said with a nod, his deep voice rich with emotion. 'I will miss him more than I can say.' Then he blinked and something skated across his eyes, something so sharp and painful she could almost feel its sting, so fleeting it was gone before she could make sense of it, even if he hadn't turned his head to look down at the grave.

Remembering, she assumed, as she studied his profile and catalogued the changes time had wrought. He had always been on the outer edge of good-looking, his dark, strong features organised in a way that was compelling rather than handsome in any conventional sense, the shadows in his features hinting at unknown dangers and untold secrets.

How many nights had she lain awake imagining all those dangers, all those secrets, wishing she might one day know them all?

Age had lent him even more mystery. The angles of his jaw looked sharper. The secrets hinted at in the shadows seemed darker, his eyes more haunted. True, there were lines around his eyes, but he was simply *more*, she decided, more than he had been before. More edgy. More mysterious.

More Raoul.

And with a start she realised that, while she'd been lost in her musings, he had changed his focus and was now studying her.

Dark-as-midnight eyes scanned her face, a hint of a frown creasing his brow, and she wondered if something was wrong before he nodded, gave her another of those slight smiles and stepped away a little to look at her. 'Whatever happened to the Gabriella I used to know? The skinny girl with plaits who always had her head in a book.'

She hid her embarrassment under a laugh, secretly hoping his comments meant that he approved of how she looked now, for it seemed important somehow that he did. She had long since come to terms with the knowledge that she'd never be classically beautiful—her eyes were too large and wide, and the chin that she'd hidden under a hand for much of her early teenage years was too pointy. But it was *her* face and over the years she'd learned to accept it, if it had taken finishing school to give her the skills to emphasise her eyes and learn to like how she looked. 'She grew up, Raoul. That skinny girl was a long, long time ago.'

'It was,' he agreed, and then he paused, as if remembering another time, other bleak days filled with funerals… 'How have you been?'

She shrugged. 'Good. And sometimes not so good.' She glanced at the open grave, felt the anguish of loss bite hard and bite deep. 'But, even so, better now for seeing you.' She paused, wondering how much she could say without revealing too much of herself, and then decided simply to be honest. 'I'm so glad you're here.'

'And me.' His dark eyes looked past her. 'But you should not be alone now.'

'Oh, I'm not. Not really. Consuelo—a friend—is here. He left…' She looked around, pushing a loose tendril of hair from her face as she scanned the cemetery. 'He left to take an urgent phone call.' *That seemed to be taking for ever.* 'Probably for one of his foundations, I expect. He heads a charity for children with cancer and leukaemia. He's always on the phone chasing contributions.'

She was babbling, she knew, making excuses for him as she glanced at her watch before scanning the grounds again, wondering how he could let one of his donors keep him so long, today of all days. 'We're heading to the hotel shortly for the wake. Everyone's already there.'

She looked back up at him, suddenly fearful that this man was about to step out of her life as quickly as he had stepped back into it, leaving her with no idea when she might ever see him again. The thought of going another ten-plus years was suddenly too awful to contemplate. 'You will come, won't you? I saw you in the chapel but you'd disappeared by the time I got outside, and I thought I'd missed you. There's so much I want to talk to you about.'

He lifted a hand and pushed that wayward coil of her hair from her cheek with just the pads of his fingers, the lightest touch that sent a rush of heat pulsing through her. 'Of course I will come. It will be my pleasure.'

Breath stalled in her lungs; his fingers lingered as he coiled the strands behind her ear, as he looked down at her with those dark, dark eyes…

'Gabby!'

She blinked, registering her name, but registering even more that Raoul had still not removed his hand. His fingers curved around her neck, gently stroking her skin, warm and evocative, even as she angled her head towards Consuelo's approach. The touch of an old friend, she told herself, reaching out to someone over a shared loss; it was nothing more than that. It would be rude, an over reaction, to brush his hand away.

'Are you coming?' Consuelo asked, still metres away and frowning as his eyes shifted from one to the other, taking in the tableau. 'We're going to be late.'

'Gabriella was waiting for you, as it happens,' Raoul said, and she looked up at him, surprised. For, even if he had correctly assumed this was Consuelo, that would hardly explain the note of barely contained animosity in his words.

Consuelo didn't seem to notice. He seemed far more interested in staring at Raoul's hand where it lingered at her throat, as if just the heat from his glare would make it disappear. For the first time she wondered if maybe it had been there too long. She put her hand to his and tugged it down, but wasn't about to let him go completely, sandwiching it between her own instead. She noticed he made no move to withdraw from her completely.

'Am I missing something?' she asked, looking from one to the other, for the first time realising the similarities in the two men—and the differences. Both shared Spanish colouring, with dark eyes and hair, but that was where the similarities began and ended. Raoul was taller, broader, more imposing. He made Consuelo look almost *small*. 'Do you two know each other?'

'Consuelo and I are old friends,' Raoul uttered slowly, in a measured tone that suggested they were anything but. 'Aren't we, Consuelo?' The other man's eyes skittered with something approximating fear before he turned to Gabriella, tugging on his tie.

'Phillipa said the priest wanted to say a few words,' he said, ignoring the other man as much as it was physically able. 'He's waiting for you to arrive to begin. Now.'

'Phillipa called you?' Was that the phone call that had kept him so long? That was odd. Her friend had never before called Consuelo; Gabriella wasn't convinced Phillipa even liked him. Unless Phillipa had figured—correctly, as it turned out—that her phone would be off and that Consuelo, with his twenty-four-seven phone addiction, would be a better bet. She nodded. At least that made some kind of sense. 'Then we should go. Raoul, can we offer you a lift?'

Consuelo stepped closer alongside her, tugging at her arm. 'Look, the car's waiting. We should get going.'

Raoul smiled. 'Thank you for your kind offer, Gabriella, but I wish to have a few words with your grandfather before I make my own way.' He lifted his hand, capturing one of hers as he raised it to his mouth, pressing his warm lips to her skin, his dark eyes glancing up at her as dark tendrils of his hair fell free from his ponytail to dance around the sharp angles and shadowed recesses of his face. 'Until we meet again, Bella,' he said, using his old pet name for her, an endearment she hadn't heard in over a decade.

But he had remembered.

And then those same eyes turned to meet the other man's and somehow turned ice-cold in the interim. 'Garbas,' he said with a nod, so simply that it took Gabriella only a second to realise he'd dismissed the other man out of hand. Consuelo felt it too, for he took her hand and tugged her away.

Raoul watched them disappear along the misty path, unable to suppress a growl when Garbas looped a proprietorial arm around Gabriella's shoulders and pulled her in close.

For his benefit, he had no doubt. Umberto had been right about the hyena sniffing around, watching and waiting for his chance to strike—not that he would see a penny of Gabriella's fortune if Raoul had anything to do with it. Not now the dogs were closing in.

It hadn't taken much. He'd known there would be dirt and plenty of it if he just dug deep enough. Now he just had to sit back and wait. It wouldn't be long and then Gabriella would be safe from his clutches.

Gabriella.

Bella.

Forgotten for years, lost under the weight of time, yet still the endearment had come to him automatically, as if all he had to do was see her before it tripped from his tongue. Yet she looked so different now from the last time they had met. When had twelve years ever passed so profitably? For him, it had been a period of loss, betrayal, death and ultimately of his own self-imposed exile. For her, it seemed those years had worked some kind of magic, transforming her from a gangly child into a very beautiful woman.

They might just as well have been living on different planets.

Huddled alongside the grave, her coat lashed tightly around her slim waist, her glossy chestnut hair coiled behind her head, she had been almost unrecognisable from the child he remembered, yet he should have seen it coming. Her mother had been beautiful after all, half-English-rose, half-Italian-royalty, her father the *crème de la crème* of French aristocracy. Her heart-shaped face somehow captured the best of all of them: her mother's cat-like eyes and smooth-as-silk complexion, her father's passionate mouth. Beautiful. Fragile.

Much too good for the likes of him.

What had Umberto been thinking? Dealing with the likes of Consuelo was one thing, but why would he want to saddle his own granddaughter with a broken creature like him? Why make him promise to marry her?

"You don't have to love her!" Umberto had said.

Just as well. What would a woman like her want with his love, even if he were able to give it? And why would she waste hers on him? Why would a woman like her ever want to marry him?

And why should she have to? Consuelo would soon be history, untouchable, locked away where he could not reach her—and not even someone who saw the good in everyone would want to defend him when she discovered the truth. Raoul could just as simply deal with any other Consuelos if it came to that. He could weed out the hyenas and the jackals, the parasites who came to prey on a rich, beautiful woman.

He could take care of them all.

Except then he remembered the touch of her skin, the smooth column of her throat and the trip of her pulse under his fingertips. He remembered the press of her cheek against his palm, remembered that moment when she had looked up at him and he had imagined the impossible, had wanted the impossible. For the first time in a long time he had felt his body stirring with want.

And that knowledge shamed him.

He hadn't meant his fingers to linger. He had wanted just to establish a contact between them, as if that might help eradicate the years that lay between them. But one touch had not been enough, and when a stray strand of hair had blown free from the knot behind her head he had been unable to resist tucking it away, using the excuse of Garbas coming upon them to leave it there.

It had been worth it just to see the look of unbridled hostility in his eyes. It had been worth even more because she had felt so damned good under his fingers.

He squeezed his eyes shut on a groan. What was he thinking? She was his oldest friend's granddaughter! The last time he had seen her she had been twelve, and it didn't matter how old she was now; she was still more than a decade younger than him. And he had been charged with taking care of her, not with taking advantage of her. He was supposed to keep her safe.

By mauling her at her grandfather's grave?

He shook his head. 'I'm sorry, Umberto, but what were you thinking?' he muttered, as he stood by the grave of his friend with just the tangle of his conflicted thoughts and the mist for company. 'Why would you make me promise such a thing when no good can come of it?'

The soft, damp air swirled around him, whispering no answers, offering no solutions, and leaving him with just one truth. He had promised his dying friend it would be so.

So he would make it happen.

CHAPTER TWO

'WHAT is he doing here?' Consuelo demanded as he strode along the path like a man with the demons of hell after him. 'Why did he have to come?'

Gabriella skipped a step to keep up with him. 'Raoul is an old family friend. Of course he would be here.'

'But the way he was touching you—like he owned you. Like he meant something to you. You let him touch you!'

'We grew up together, Consuelo. Our two families were practically inseparable, at least until I was twelve years of age. The last time I saw him was at our parents' funerals. Of course there is some feeling between us. He is like a brother to me.'

He looked across at her suddenly, his eyes wild and frantic, and she wondered what else must be troubling him for him to overreact in this way. 'And that's all he is to you?'

'But of course,' she said, wanting to soothe, but mostly because there was nothing else she could say, even if she might so foolishly have once dreamed of more.

He wrapped his arm around her shoulders and tugged

her close in to his body. She needed to be hugged but she wondered why this contact didn't stir her blood or warm her as Raoul's touch had done. Perhaps because she saw more of him, or because he was more familiar to her, more comfortable to be around. She shouldn't encourage him—she knew he wanted more out of their relationship than she could commit to right now—but today she was glad to have someone to hold on to, even if his touch didn't stir her like another's...

She shuddered now with the memory of it, of how just the gentle touch of Raoul's fingertips had set her blood fizzing. How was that possible—a man she hadn't met other than in her dreams for so many years? Or had she just wished and hoped for it so much, she'd believed it had happened?

But then he'd always had that impact on her. He'd always seemed larger than life, and she'd always been drawn to his dark mystery. Why should it be any different now, simply because a dozen years had passed?

'How do you know Raoul?' she asked, curious as he hastened her towards the waiting car. 'Is he one of the foundation's benefactors?'

He laughed, a short, derisive laugh. 'Him? No, he would not give to a charity such as ours, not even to save the lives of sick children.'

'Why do you say that? Have you ever asked him?'

'I do not bother with his sort. His kind have no heart.'

'No, Consuelo,' she protested, remembering back, thinking that Raoul had had the biggest heart of anyone she knew. Nothing had been too much trouble for him back then, nothing too much effort for his family and hers. And when the police had called that fateful evening with the shocking news it had been Raoul who had cradled her, letting her cry her eyes out, offering her the remnants of his own shattered heart. 'That cannot be right.'

'Then you do not know him very well, after all. Come,' he said, opening her car door so she could precede him into the vehicle. 'Forget Raoul; there are more important things to think about right now.' He tapped the waiting driver on the shoulder to let him know they were ready. 'Like arranging for your things to be moved from the house into my apartment. Given you're on leave, it would be the perfect time.'

She blinked, momentarily stunned. Where had that come from? 'What are you talking about?'

But he was engrossed in the traffic, scanning it, almost as if he was looking for someone. Raoul? Surely he was a long way behind. And then he turned back to her, smiling, and she wondered if she'd imagined his nervousness. 'Come on, darling. Now that your grandfather's gone, there's no reason why we should live apart any longer.'

'We haven't talked about this.'

He took her hand in one of his, patted it with the other. 'Come, Gabby, you know as well as I do that half the reason you haven't moved in already is because your grandfather needed you. Now there is no reason for us to be apart. Now it is time you were looked after the way you should be. The way I want to look after you.'

She shook her head. 'Consuelo…'

'Of course, I can always move in with you, but I

thought you might prefer a fresh start somewhere else, somewhere without the memories.'

'I like where I live,' she said, stiffening and wondering what she had said or done to make him think she was ready to move in with him. 'And my grandfather is barely cold in his grave. I would actually prefer not to have to deal with this today.'

He sighed and lifted her hand to his lips, although his eyes lacked any warmth to go with it. 'I'm sorry, Gabby. I'm rushing you. Of course we can talk later.'

Much later, she thought, clutching her coat at her neck and wondering what it was that was throwing Consuelo so off-kilter today; he was so very anxious as he resumed his busy scanning of the traffic.

They were almost at the hotel when Consuelo's phone buzzed again. He pulled it from his pocket and held it to his ear, and Gabriella looked across, wondering if it was Phillipa again wanting to know how far away they were. But even as she watched the colour drained from Consuelo's face.

'Mierda!' he said, before he snapped it off and shoved it away, tapping the driver on the shoulder. 'Stop here. Let me out here.'

'Consuelo, what's wrong?' she asked as the driver cut across two lanes of traffic, to the squeal of tyres and the blare of horns, to double park on the side of the road. 'Who was that?'

But he was already climbing out. 'A problem at the office. I have to go.' And then he slammed the door and disappeared into the crowd.

* * *

The priest's words were moving, the condolences she received from old friends and associates heartfelt, and Gabriella felt one kind of peace descend on her soul. Her grandfather had been much loved by all who had known him, had touched so many lives, and it was clear that it wasn't just her who would be left with an Umberto-sized hole in her heart.

But now the wake was winding down and she felt suddenly deflated with it. She'd turned her phone on to silent, hoping that she might get some news from Consuelo, some kind of explanation, but there had been no messages explaining his sudden disappearance or when he might join her. She was beginning to think he wouldn't make it at all.

And maybe she could have lived with that if Raoul had bothered to turn up like he'd promised. She'd hoped he'd soon follow them from the cemetery. From the very first minute she'd stepped into the hotel's plush recep-tion-room, she'd been anticipating his arrival, scanning the room for a hint of his broad, dark-clad shoulders or a glimpse of his blue-black hair. She longed for the dark solidity of his presence. She longed for the comfort she'd found in it at the cemetery, a comfort she yearned for now.

He'd promised he'd come. She ached with wanting him to come. So where was he?

Phillipa appeared at her side and put a hand on her shoulder. 'How are you bearing up?'

'Do men always let you down?' she mused as she stared blankly into a cold cup of coffee in her hands that she battled to remember picking up. First Umberto, the grandfather who had taken her in as a grieving twelve-year-old and had been both mother and father to her, was gone. Then Consuelo, who couldn't even stop thinking about his foundation for just one day, disappeared to who knew where and for how long? And now Raoul, who she'd lost before she'd even found again.

'Hey, don't worry,' said Phillipa. 'You know how he is,' she continued, clearly only seeing one side to Gabriella's concerns. Her friend squeezed her hand as she prised the neglected cup from her fingers. 'The foundation is everything to him. He's got caught up in something, that's all. And, for the record, men don't always let you down. Not all of them, at any rate.'

'I'm sorry,' she said, remembering Phillipa's gorgeous husband. 'I'm just feeling maudlin. You have a keeper of a man. He is a wonder to bring you all the way from London just for me and with such a young baby.'

She kissed Gabriella's cheek. 'Nothing is too much trouble for you, but you're right; Damien is a keeper, but he will need rescuing from our baby soon. Will you be all right if I leave?'

'I'll be fine. You've been so wonderful today. Oh, and I meant to say before, thanks for calling while we were at the cemetery. I lost track of time completely out there.'

Her friend looked blank.

'You phoned Consuelo,' Gabriella prompted. 'To tell him the priest was waiting for me to begin his talk.'

Phillipa frowned and shook her head. 'I never called. I don't even have his number.' It was Gabriella's turn to blink. Why had Consuelo made out that she had? Unless he'd been so desperate to get her away from Raoul that he'd resorted to lies to do it. What had happened between the two men that nobody was letting on about?

Phillipa put a hand on her elbow. 'Gabriella, are you okay?'

Suddenly it was too hard to think. She put a hand on her brow. 'I'm sorry. I've got a rotten headache. I must have misunderstood.' Her friend smiled and squeezed her arm.

'Let me get you some painkillers and some water. It might take the edge off it.'

Gabriella sighed, letting herself sag, hidden for a moment behind a marble pillar, trying desperately to relax. Her head hurt. Her feet ached. And her heart felt like a giant void. If only she could take a pill for that. Today she'd said goodbye to her grandfather, the man who had taken on the role of both her parents and more when they had been ripped from her life. Such a good man. Such a brilliant man. Why did the world—why did she—have to live without him just yet?

She looked around the room, looking at the few remaining guests talking over their coffee and cognac, wondering if anyone would notice if she simply disappeared. But she was kidding herself. Of course she couldn't just slip away. She would have to stay until the grim and bitter end.

Then the air in the room seemed to still and intensify until it shimmered with expectation. The hairs at the back of her neck stood up as she felt the scorching gaze of dark eyes drinking her in. Phillipa joined her, blinking as she held out a glass of sparkling water—not that she was looking at Gabriella. 'Oh, wow, forget keeper husbands for a moment. Who on earth is that?'

Gabriella didn't have to turn around to know who it was. She could feel his identity in her rapidly liquefying bones. She could feel it in her heated flesh and empty lungs.

He had come.

And then he was beside them, so broad, tall and dangerous-looking that his presence should darken the world, except that it only served to brighten hers.

'Raoul Del Arco,' he said, bowing to her friend. 'At your service.' Although it was the fingers pressed to the small of her back that had Gabriella's full attention, the press of them against her flesh sending an electrical current surging along her spine, needles of sensation that radiated out to take anchor in the suddenly sensitive tissue of her breasts and dark places inside, deep down in her belly.

'I thought you weren't coming,' she said a little breathlessly when she'd managed to unglue her tongue from where it had been stuck to the roof of her mouth. And then, because she realised it sounded like it contained a note of desperation and even accusation, she forced herself to smile. 'But thank you for coming now. And let me introduce Phillipa Edwards. We went to the same boarding school in England.'

Raoul nodded, taking her hand. 'It is a pleasure.'

'Raoul was like a big brother to me growing up,' she continued. *And my personal hero.*

'Umberto was a very important influence in my life and Gabriella has always been very special to me,' he said as his arm moved upwards, his long-fingered hand cupping her shoulder, pulling her close against his heated body, a gesture that seemed a world away from brotherly, at least the heated way her body seemed to be interpreting it. 'Unfortunately we lost touch for several years, so to meet again under such circumstances makes for a bittersweet reunion.' He looked down at her, his dark eyes intense, mesmerising. 'I see now I will have to ensure I do not allow such a lapse to occur again.'

Clearly she should have eaten, because she felt dizzy at his words, so light-headed that she could have fallen into his eyes right then and there if Phillipa had not excused herself, saying she needed to get back to her baby. Gabriella hugged her friend and then she was alone with Raoul.

He dropped his arm to face her; absurdly she missed his touch and the warm solidity of his body pressed against hers. Then he tilted his dark head and smiled in a way that transformed his features from darkly threatening to something warm and dangerous that could melt cement as easily as it could buckle her knees. 'I am sorry to have kept you waiting, Bella. You said you wanted to talk and I felt that might prove easier after everyone had gone. I thought, I hoped, you might allow me to take you to dinner.'

Bella.

There was that name again.

'I was just going to go home.'

'Ah, but of course.' He looked around the room, the remaining stragglers exchanging stories and talking over old times. 'It has been a very long day for you. Then maybe I can take you home?'

'No, not home,' she decided suddenly. At home there would be no treasured grandfather waiting for her, ever again. Why had she ever thought 'home' would offer some kind of sanctuary?

Besides, with Raoul beside her she didn't feel so enervated, so drained. Instead, it seemed like every nerve ending in her body was suddenly awake and acutely aware of the man before her.

And acutely aware of a sudden hunger. It felt like she hadn't eaten for ever. 'Thank you, Raoul. If the offer still stands, dinner would be lovely.'

He stayed by her side while the wake wound up, lending her his strength when mourners departed and succumbed to a final burst of tears as they kissed her goodbye, and then he took her to a tiny 1890's bistro on the Left Bank that greeted them with the scent of roasted garlic and tomatoes, with its *belle epoque* decor, quaint etched-glass and globe lamps. It was not somewhere she'd been expecting to be taken and definitely somewhere she was sure Consuelo would not know existed. There were no billionaires here that she could see, no players, politicians or film stars. Simply ordinary people enjoying a night out.

Well, ordinary apart from Raoul. There was nothing ordinary about his broad shoulders and strong black hair that glowed blue in the subtle lighting. He shrank the tiny room with his sheer presence, blotting out the other diners until they might just as well have been cardboard cut-outs. It felt good to be able to sit opposite and have no reason not to look at him and drink in his strong features—those dark eyes with their depths only hinted at under that dark slash of brow; those sculpted cheekbones, strong blade of nose and those lips, their passionate lines as detailed as if chiselled by a sculptor's hand.

It felt good to be here with him.

'Twice today I have found you alone,' he said after they had ordered their meals. 'Could Garbas not stay until the end of the wake?'

She fiddled with the napkin in her lap. Consuelo hadn't made it at all, not that Raoul needed to know that, not when he clearly harboured enough resentment towards the man already. And not when there had been no word and she still had no idea herself what was going on. 'He was called away. Something important, I guess.'

'More important than you?'

She flushed and waited while the waiter poured them both a glass of Beaujolais, ruby red in the light cast by the lamp in the centre of the table. Consuelo always had good reasons when he was delayed or had to suddenly change their plans—it happened so often that she was used to it. To let her down today of all days… But he would have good reason, she was sure.

Although, what reason would he have for assuming they would now move in together?

She picked up her glass on a sigh, admiring the colour of the wine. Maybe he'd just felt neglected, with her attention going firstly to her grandfather and then to Phillipa when she'd needed her recently. And maybe he hadn't been uppermost in her thoughts these last few weeks and wanted to change that. But, still, when had

going to a few parties and dinners together been a sign
of imminent cohabitation?

Then she saw Raoul waiting for her and decided to
worry about the missing Consuelo and his distorted per-
ception of their relationship later. She gave an ironic
smile. 'Clearly much more important. Anyway, I didn't
come to dinner to talk about him.'

'Touché.' Across the table Raoul smiled and lifted his
glass to hers in a toast. 'To us, Gabriella. To old friends
and new beginnings.'

His words stirred her soul deep. 'To us,' she said, taking a sip, feeling the sensual slide of fine wine down her
throat. She watched him watching her over the rim of
her glass, liking the way he watched her, wondering if
he liked what he saw.

And she knew she was in danger of reading too much
into this. She was feeling things and hearing things that
couldn't possibly be there or mean what she thought.
And for all his talk of new beginnings and expressions
of regret that it had been so long, he would most likely
disappear from her life tonight and not even Umberto
would be there to bring him back to her.

After all, this was Raoul, and her teenaged fantasies
had been just that—fantasies. She put her glass down
before the alcohol might convince her otherwise. 'You
visited Umberto the week before he died?'

Across the table Raoul stilled. 'Umberto told you
that?'

She shook her head and the lights in her hair danced
under the lamps. She'd worn it up for the funeral, a severe knot at the back of her head, but time and the damp

had worked tendrils loose, so now the ends softly framed her face. 'No, his nurse. He died before—before I made it home from London. I was too late to see him.'

'I'm sorry,' he said, praying that his visit had done nothing to hasten his old friend's death and prevent his granddaughter one last opportunity to see him.

'I think he knew he was dying and he didn't want me there.' She looked at the ceiling and pressed her lips together in a thin white line. 'He sent me away, you know.'

'I didn't know.'

'Phillipa was almost due to give birth. Her husband was overseas and booked to get back—there should have been plenty of time—when a coup closed all the airports. He was stuck in a war zone and she was frantic with worry; little wonder the baby came early. And I didn't want to leave Umberto, but he told me he was fine and that I must go to help my friend. He promised me he would be fine...'

He took her hand, squeezed it in his own. 'He was looking out for you. He was trying to spare you.'

'By denying me the opportunity to share his final days, his final moments?' She hauled in a breath and shook her head. 'Why don't I feel blessed in that case? Instead, I feel cheated. I didn't even get a proper chance to say goodbye.'

'Bella,' he said, his hand stroking her cheek, his thumb wiping the moisture welling from her eyes, 'He didn't want you to see him like that.'

'But why wouldn't he want to say goodbye to me?'

'Because maybe he wanted you to remember him as he was before, strong and happy, not confined to a bed with a battery of machines beeping out his existence while you waited for them to fall silent one by one. He loved you too much to subject you to that.'

She sniffed and rested her cheek against his hand, staring blindly at the table as if considering his words. She looked lost, a little girl in a woman's face, a little girl who had suffered too much already in her short life; a beautiful face that was no hardship to stare at, no hardship to caress. Even with leaking eyes and tear-streaked cheeks, even with that trembling bottom lip, she was indeed a beauty. Even without her fortune in waiting, she would be a catch.

What a waste.

For she deserved only the best. She deserved happiness and love and a good man who could give her both.

She deserved so much more than a man who would marry her simply to fulfil the terms of a promise.

And that wretched knot he seemed to endlessly carry with him grew in his gut, twisting, tangling and pulling tight. Why was he even considering going through with this? Garbas would be no threat now. Garbas could not hurt her. So he should just take her home, say goodnight and walk away. He should let her go. If he had any sense at all, he would just let her go. Umberto would never know.

Except he had promised.

And *he* would know.

Besides, perversely perhaps, a part of him was beginning to think it would not be such an impossible feat to get her to agree to marry him. Indeed, the longer he was with her, the more certain he was that he could achieve the unthinkable. She had worshipped him as a child. She certainly didn't hate him now, not from the way she seemed to lean into his touch, not from the way he found her glancing at him when she thought he wasn't looking. And, whatever she'd heard of his past, it didn't seem to make her wary of him in any way. *Foolish, foolish woman.*

'So what did he say?'

He looked up to find her eyes on him, sad eyes wanting answers.

'You talked to Umberto,' she prompted. 'What did he say?'

He hesitated, his hand dropping, his fingers toying with the stem of his wine glass, knowing what her reaction would be if he told her what Umberto really wanted from him.

'Surely I'm entitled to know something of his last words? Can't you tell me anything?'

'*Si.*' He nodded. 'Of course you are entitled. Because mostly, Bella, he talked of you.'

'Me.' She blinked and swallowed and he followed the movement down the long, smooth column of her throat until it disappeared into her chest, a slow, sensual slide. He had to drag his eyes north again when she said, 'What did he say about me?'

'That he loved you,' he said, embellishing the truth, because he knew she needed to hear it and because he knew it to be true. 'More than anything or anyone in the world. He talked about how special you are and how much you mean to him. He talked about how afraid he was for you when he was gone, how he would miss seeing you married with children one day.'

She dragged in air and bit down on her plump bottom lip with her teeth in the way he remembered her always doing whenever she'd been upset years ago. He remembered her trying not to cry out loud at her parents' funeral and biting down so hard on her lip those teeth had drawn blood, blood she'd later smeared on his white shirt when he'd hugged her and held her close. How her twelve-year-old's tears had reduced him to tears too, even though he'd promised himself to be strong that day.

God, but she'd been through so much. He could well understand Umberto wanting to protect her and ensure nothing bad ever happened to her again. He wanted that too. And, the longer he was with her, the more he wanted it. But he still knew in his crusted heart that he was the last person who could make it so.

'He told me that you see the good in everyone, that you do not judge, that you have a good heart.'

Across the table, she sniffed. 'Thank you. It would have been nice to have heard these things first hand, but it is good to hear them at all, so thank you.'

'Sometimes it is not possible to say these things face to face. Your grandfather was old-school. Did he ever tell you he loved you when he was alive?'

'No, but I still knew.'

'Yes, you knew. Some things, Bella—some things do not need to be said for us to know them to be true,' he said, feeling only slightly guilty for the things he'd told her, the things he'd embellished and the things he'd omitted when he saw how happy she was to hear them.

And she smiled, tears once again welling in her eyes. 'Thank you, Raoul,' she said as she clasped his hand in hers, only letting go as their meals were served. 'Thank you so much.'

CHAPTER THREE

'WHAT will you do now?' he asked while they ate. 'Will you stay in Paris?'

She tilted her head as she toyed with a mushroom, contemplating his question and letting herself appreciate for the first time just how much she was enjoying tonight. She hadn't expected to enjoy anything today, and there was still an Umberto-sized hole in her chest. But she felt, if not entirely happy, then almost *good*, she decided, although she was in no doubt that the company was a major factor in that. Just being with Raoul seemed to make her feel good, to feel warm.

'I have my job at the American Library here in Paris. They've given me leave, as long as I need, although I think I really should get back to work. I've been off more than a month already.'

'You don't look like any librarian I've ever seen,' he offered. 'In fact, if librarians had looked like you when I was at school, I might have spent more time studying in the library.'

She smiled and tilted her head. 'Why thank you, kind sir, but I think perhaps that is the wine talking.'

'No,' he countered. 'That is definitely the man talking.'

She felt his words in the quake that rumbled its way down her spine and lodged deep in her belly; she had to suck in air to cool and mitigate its far-flung effects. 'I'm the special-collections manager,' she said, squeezing her legs together under the table to quell the buzzing between her thighs. 'Maybe the library gods give us a bit more leeway in that department.'

And to her relief he laughed, a rich, deep sound that resonated through her bones. 'Come to Venice with me.'

Her breath caught—or maybe it was her heart—and it was her turn to laugh, but this time nervously. 'Excuse me?'

'I have business in Venice. Come with me, Bella.'

She shook her head, once again blindsided by the events of the day. She was torn to think he was leaving already after such a short time, tempted to do something wildly un-Gabriella-like and take off with him. But she didn't work that way. 'I can't just take off to Venice.'

'Why not?'

'I have my job.'

'You're on leave.'

'But… But…' She was thinking of all the reasons going to Venice with Raoul would be so wonderful: the chance to renew their acquaintance, the opportunity to feel his warming presence; logic momentarily deserted her.

'What do you have to stay for? A change would do you good.'

When he put it like that, it *had* been a long time

since she'd had any kind of holiday. Once she went back to work it would be months before she could ask for more time off, and the thought of going to Venice with Raoul… 'No.' She shook her head, much more emphatically this time, half to convince herself. 'That's silly. What were we talking about again?'

He shrugged, as if it didn't matter one way or the other. 'So, think about it. No rush. Meanwhile, we were talking about you. Where did you go to school? I seem to remember Umberto mentioning boarding school once or twice when I visited him.'

She nodded, feeling warmed by the thought of Umberto talking to Raoul about his granddaughter and what she was doing—and Raoul actually remembering—while in the back of her mind she kept hearing his words, *Come with me, Bella.*

She took a sip of water, wondering if it was the wine making her feel reckless enough to want to say yes. Then she marshalled her scattered thoughts enough to answer his question properly.

'From the day I was born, my mother had me booked into the same ladies college in the Cotswolds she'd attended as a girl. I'd always known I was going there and, while I didn't want to leave Umberto, it felt good being there and nearer her parents, too, while they were alive. And I'd see Mum's name on winners' boards and amongst lists of past prefects and it made me feel good—walking those same corridors, sitting in those same classrooms that she had. Like I was closer to her, if that makes any sense.'

Suddenly she wasn't sure what made sense and

what didn't. She gave a nervous laugh, tilted her head. 'Did you actually mean it about coming to Venice?' Immediately she dismissed it. 'But, no, sorry, it's a crazy idea. I'm probably not making any sense.'

'You make perfect sense,' he said, raising his glass to her. 'And it's not such a crazy idea.'

Oh, but it was. If she went to Venice she might get used to the warm, wonderful way he made her feel—as if she had one hundred per cent of his attention all the time, as if she were the only person, the only woman, in the world.

And that would be crazy.

'Anyway,' she pressed on, determined to get back to her story and not dwell on things that could not be, 'That's where I met Phillipa.'

'Your friend I met today?'

She nodded, remembering the first day they'd met, the two girls who'd teamed up in desperation because they'd known nobody else in the entire school and yet had stayed friends ever since. 'She was my very best friend from day one, even through the couple of years when her family shifted to New York. She came back to study librarianship at uni as well, and we ended up living together during terms. We'd each go our separate ways in the holidays, her to New York, me to Paris, or we'd take turns at visiting each other's homes.' She smiled. 'Phillipa's the most brilliant friend. Better than a sister—not that I've ever had one.'

She stopped, and looked at him, leaning back and smiling patiently at her. 'Oh God, I'm talking too much, aren't I?'

'No, I could listen to you all night. I wish I had been there more for you, Bella.' Maybe if he had, he wouldn't have ended up so lost himself… 'I should have done more.'

She shrugged. 'Come on, Raoul, how could you? The last thing you needed was to be bothered with a girl barely in her teens. And I was fine. I actually liked boarding school. It was hard at first, but in a way it took my mind off things. Besides, what could you have done? You were busy with your own life.'

Busy? That was one way to put it. And, realistically, what could he have done? He'd spent the two years after his parents' death either drunk or aiming for it, playing every casino he could find, throwing money at every game and every horse it was possible to lose on and finding himself a new family into the deal. A family that loved someone who could splash money around and not care, a family who had adopted him for one of their own, if only to suck him dry.

And then, emerging out of the bleakness of that time, he'd found Katia—or she had found him. Playboy of the year, bachelor of the year; he'd been awarded so many of those meaningless titles he couldn't remember them all. But she had wanted him above all others and they had been so absorbed in their own special world that nothing else had mattered. Or so he had thought. Not until much later when the foundations of his world had once again been torn apart…

He shook his head, wondering at the insanity that had driven his actions then, knowing he should know better now. For it had to be a form of insanity to be contemplating what he was doing, to be undertaking what he was doing.

Even now he'd primed Gabriella perfectly; she was still thinking about Venice even though he'd said nothing to encourage her after that first exchange. Even now she was still thinking it through, working out the angles, making it possible in her own mind, making it her own decision.

Even now it could still happen—and he could get her to Venice and clear of Paris before the news of Consuelo's inevitable arrest broke. For Consuelo would be arrested, nothing was surer.

But right now, looking into Gabriella's eyes flickering brandy-gold in the lamplight, he wasn't so sure of anything else. The way she looked at him…

She wasn't the girl she had once been. She was a woman now, and his body was reacting the way a man's body did to a woman he desired.

He shook his head, trying to dispel those images. 'You were no doubt better off without me.' *As you would be now.*

She reached over, took his hands in hers. 'I'm sorry. How about we make a deal? How about we don't think about the past? Maybe it's time we let it go. You yourself toasted to a new beginning, so can't we just leave it at that? Can we let the past go and start again?'

If only it were that easy!

His past *was* him. It was his past that had made him, shaped him and moulded him, even broken him along the way. It had made him who he was now.

How could he let that go without losing himself, without losing who he was now?

He didn't know how.

He wouldn't know where to begin.

And, promise or no promise, suddenly he couldn't do this—not to himself and definitely not to her. It was suddenly too hot, the air like poison as the walls of the bistro closed in on him. He knew he had to get outside into the fresh air, into a world where he could disappear and be alone and where she would be safe from him.

'Are you finished?' he asked, already standing, his voice like gravel as he threw some notes onto the table.

She blinked up at him in surprise, grabbing her coat as he moved like a dark cloud past her out of the restaurant and into the night.

It was raining, the lamps along the Seine throwing jagged zigzags of colour sliding along the wet pavement and across the dark water. 'Raoul,' she said, as she skipped to keep up with his long stride. 'What's wrong? What did I say?'

'It is nothing you have said, nothing you have done.'

'Then, what?'

'It is me, Gabriella.' It stung like a slap to her face that he had dropped the use of Bella, dropped the endearment. 'You are better off without me.'

'No, Raoul, how can you say that?'

'Because I know! You were right to decide not to come with me.'

He hailed a taxi and bundled her and she thought he would follow until he rattled off her address and made to close the door. She threw out her hand against the door to stop him. 'What are you doing?'

'Sending you home. Good bye, Gabriella.'

She shoved open the door and stood up to him, face to face, the door—and a world, it seemed—between them. 'No. Not until I know when I will see you again.'

'You do not want to see me again.'

'Don't tell me what I want!' There was a spark in her eyes he hadn't seen before, a hint of rebellion about that sharp chin he hadn't seen since she was a child. Not that it would do her any good.

The driver uttered a few impatient words and she turned and let go with a torrent of French of her own before she turned back. 'I don't want to wait another twelve years to see you again, and I damn well won't.'

'Who can say how long it will be?'

'So, what time do you leave? We could still meet for lunch if it's late enough.'

'No.'

'Then maybe breakfast at your hotel?'

'That is not possible. I leave mid-morning.'

'Can't you change it?'

'I told you, I have business to attend to.'

'And it cannot wait?'

'No.'

Infuriating! He was like a mountain made out of a single piece of solid granite, She could pound her fists against his chest except she knew he would not feel a thing. 'Then maybe I was too hasty before. Maybe I could come with you after all, even just for a day or two. Like you say, the library will not expect me back immediately.'

'I'm sorry, Gabriella, but I was too hasty with my invitation. I should have realised it would not work.'

'But you asked me. Why would you do that? Why would you ask and then change your mind?'

'Because it is pointless! Because I cannot do this—please do not try to make me.'

'For God's sake, Raoul, you blast into my life after a twelve-year absence and then you disappear before we've had a chance to get to know each other again. Can't you at least offer me something?

'But I am, Bella—I am offering you your freedom. Treasure it.'

And he turned and strode off into the wet, dark Paris night.

She watched him go, wishing she could run after him, knowing it would be a mistake. But what had he meant about offering her her freedom? Why should she treasure it?

Why couldn't he at least have explained what he meant?

He dreamed of Katia that night, Katia emerging from the mist with all her grace and long, lithe limbs, her dancer's eyes and beckoning smile. He dreamed of parties floating on a champagne cloud; he dreamed of laughter, dancing and sex that went long into the night and the following day, and then doing it all again the next. Until the mist turned dark and putrid and a mocking smile became a call for help, became a scream, and he tried to make his feet move, tried to run…

He woke to a pounding heart, covered in sweat and tangled in sheets. It took seconds to realise the pounding was coming from the door and not only from his chest. Thank God! He swung his legs over the side of the bed and sat up, snatching up his watch and throwing it back when he saw the time and realised it had taken him so long to get to sleep last night that he'd slept later than he'd intended. It was room service, no doubt, with his breakfast order, although why they had to make such a God-awful noise…

He called out that he was coming and lashed a towel around his hips, pulling open the door in the same movement. But it was Gabriella who fell into his arms, tear-streaked and brandishing a newspaper in one hand, and it took him a moment to remember, to work out how she'd found him. 'Raoul, I'm sorry,' she sobbed, clinging to him. 'I'm so sorry. I know you'll be angry with me, but I didn't know who else to turn to.'

He put a tentative hand to her head, trying not to think too much about the push of her breasts again his chest or the fact his early-morning body had reversed its decision to relax. Hating himself that it had. 'What is it, Gabriella?' he asked gruffly, shifting slightly and still feeling a building sizzle of satisfaction in his veins, already half-knowing what the news must be.

'It's all over the papers,' she sniffed, thrusting it into his hand. 'It's Consuelo. He's been accused of using the foundation as a front for money laundering. He's been arrested for fraud.'

Already? he thought as his eyes flicked over the article, taking in the pertinent details. So it was done and she was safe. Surely Umberto would not quibble about the exact letter of his promise not being carried out? He'd done her a favour, after all, and if all went to plan Garbas would be locked up for a very long time and Gabriella could find and marry someone decent. 'But what brings you here? What do you think I can do?'

'We have to help him. It can't be true. We have to—'

'We?'

'Surely you would help me?'

'But if it is true, what they accuse him of?'

She blinked watery eyes up at him and exhilaration almost gave way to regret for causing her more tears after she had shed what seemed like an ocean of them. 'What?'

'If the police are right? That he has been using the foundation as a front?'

She buried her head against his chest again, as if to block out the truth. 'But that would make him some kind of criminal.'

'Then maybe, just maybe, you should brace yourself for that eventuality.'

She stilled in his arms. 'You think there is a possibility?'

He shrugged, unable to prevent himself from stroking her back through her coat, trying to show indifference when all he wanted to do was tell her that he knew it to be true and that she had had a lucky escape. Could she not tell from the gravity of the reports that this was no frame-up? Then battling to care about Garbas and whether he was guilty or innocent when she was in his arms this way, and so very beautiful, so very desirable…

With a groan, he hauled his libido and his thoughts back to where they should be.

'The police must have evidence. They do not go around arresting people on such charges lightly, Bella.'

The use of her pet name sliced through her tears and through the dense fog that had occupied her mind ever since he had abandoned her last night, leaving her sleepless and unable to cope with this morning's revelations.

And suddenly she was aware of so many other things—of the spring of chest hair under her fingers; of the broad width of naked chest that lay heated under her cheek and pressed against her breasts; of the rough towel that was the only barrier separating them.

'You called me Bella,' she said, lifting her head to look up at him. 'I thought you hated me.'

He stroked her hair back from her face. 'I could never hate you.'

And she smiled. 'Nor me you. I think we are destined to be friends for ever, Raoul.' Even though, with his warm, firm flesh under her hands, she wished it could be more.

He kissed the top of her head. 'I believe so. I'm sorry I was so—abrupt last night, Bella. There are things you do not understand.'

'I would be happy to try, if only you would let me.'

He let her go and turned away, so suddenly that she was left to find her balance in a world that had somehow subtly shifted while she was in his arms. 'I should get dressed,' he said, opening his wardrobe. 'So, what do you intend to do?'

It took her a moment to work out what he meant. 'I have to do something. Maybe I should go to the police station—tell them there must be another explanation. Offer to be a character witness.'

Halfway pulling out a shirt from a wardrobe, he stopped and looked at her. 'Do you always believe the best of people, Bella? Always? No matter what?'

It was her turn to shrug. 'But how can it be true? The foundation does such wonderful work. I have seen the children he has helped—tiny children with no hope until his foundation funds their treatment; tiny children who have lost so much and yet are still able to smile because of what his foundation has done for them—offering them hope for some kind of future. What will happen to them?'

He growled as he shrugged the shirt on. Was she so naive that she couldn't see that Consuelo's purpose was to hide behind those very children he pretended to care about in order to cover his filthy tracks? 'They will not suffer because of this.'

She shook her head. 'I don't know. I keep thinking someone must have made a mistake. Maybe it's someone working for him behind the scenes who might have done this. And I can't help feeling there must be something I can do to help.'

His fingers stabbed the last shirt-button home, his blood running cold in his veins while he watched her over his shoulder. 'Do you love him, Bella—this man who abandoned you yesterday on a day you needed

friends to stand by you? Is that why you are so desperate to help him?'

'No.' She made a sound like a whimper. 'No, but does
it have to be about love? He's a friend, and he's going to
need all the friends he can to get through this.'

'And yesterday, when you needed a friend? Where
was he then, if not already running, if what the paper
suggests is true? Why else would his offices be raided?
Why else would he have been arrested at the airport like
that article says if he was not trying to flee? Unless he
had plans to travel that you knew about?'

'No.' She squeezed her eyes shut. 'We were planning
on having a quiet dinner together.'

'Then how much help do you think you can be, without proving him to be a liar with your evidence?'

She collapsed on the un-made bed, her face in her
hands. 'I'm sorry. I don't know! I just don't know what
to do.'

She looked so vulnerable and broken, so desperate
and despair-ridden, that he could not help but feel guilty,
even when Garbas was scum and had it coming to him.
There was little triumph here. In kicking Garbas, he'd
kicked her too when she was already down, even if it
was to save her.

But there was no way now he would walk away and
leave her here in Paris, not like this. All she knew was
death and loss here, and a friend she was determined
to defend. She was just as likely to go to the police and
ask to speak to him. If she asked him if he had done it
and Garbas said he had not, of course she would believe

him. She would never be free of him, not really, not unless…

God, what a mess.

'Bella,' he said, sitting alongside her, pulling her into his arms. 'I will tell you what you must do. You must pack your bags and come with me to Venice and you will forget all about what is happening here.'

She sniffed again against his chest, a fresh torrent of tears hot against his fresh shirt. 'But you don't want me there,' she sobbed. 'You said you didn't.'

'I'm asking you now.'

'So why now and not last night? You didn't want me to come last night. You sent me home.'

He sighed, stroking her hair, looking across the room at nothing in particular. 'Last night I was reminded of things I would rather forget. Not because of you, Bella, but Umberto's death reached me in places I did not want to go. And I was angry. Unthinking. Careless of your feelings. But I cannot leave you here like this in Paris, all alone, with Umberto gone and your friend in jail.'

She shook her head. 'But…'

He took her chin in his hand and lifted it so he could see her eyes. 'You have leave. Why not make the most of it? How long has it been since you had a real holiday?'

Too long, if the lost look in her eyes was any indication. 'You said it has been years since you were in Venice,' he said, knowing she was swayed. 'I have an apartment on a canal, big enough that I could do my work and you could sightsee to your heart's content. And we could sip wine in the evening on the balcony and watch the gondolas slip by. What do you say?'

Her eyes swirled with the possibilities. He saw them; he saw her hesitation and felt her temptation as she tasted the opportunity before her. And still she wavered. 'I don't know.'

'Of course you do,' he said. 'And then in a few weeks, when all this has all settled down and you are feeling stronger, come back and see what you can do for your friend then. Maybe it will have all blown over. But things will be clearer then, I know.'

She looked up at him, and he could see she was torn. 'You really think so?'

'I know so.'

Her teeth found her lip—swollen and bruised from yesterday's stresses he realised—and he put a thumb to her lip if only to stop her injuring herself further. 'You've hurt yourself. Don't do that.' And even as he brushed her lips apart with his finger she looked up at him with those wide cat's eye. Even though he knew it was folly, even though he knew it could lead nowhere good, he could not resist. So he dipped his mouth to hers, tentatively, whisperingly soft, no more than a brush of skin against skin.

Yet she shuddered against him like the world had quaked beneath her feet.

My doing, he thought with a touch of satisfaction as he tasted her lips and felt the foundations of his own soul shift and stir and bring him reluctantly to awareness— where he had no intention of going.

He returned the finger to her lips, pushing himself away, reminding himself why he was doing this. He would have to kiss her, he told himself, if this was to work. It meant nothing. And then, once she was safe, he could let her go. She would be free to find someone worthy of her, someone who could offer her a future filled with life and love.

She looked up at him, all blinking eyes and breathlessness, her lips parted as if she could not draw in enough air any other way, as if waiting for him to kiss her again.

Later, he thought, knowing he shouldn't rush her, knowing he should take his time. Because he had no choice, even though it was the wrong choice. He couldn't leave her here.

Because, like it or not, Umberto had been right all the time.

There was no other way.

CHAPTER FOUR

VENICE enchanted her. From the moment she first caught sight of their destination as their plane came into land at Marco Polo airport, Gabriella was struck by the soft beauty of this ageing city perched upon the sea. From the air it had looked like a fantasy land, seemingly floating atop the waters of the lagoon, the tell-tale S of the grand canal slicing through its many islands.

From the *vaporetto* as they approached the city, it appeared even more magical. She sighed with pleasure, soaking up the soft sun on her bare arms, the breeze dancing through her hair. It felt like for ever since she'd felt the sun's kiss on her skin or the whispering breeze in her hair and she tossed her head back, letting her hair flick and dance on the warm air.

There was something exotic and timeless about approaching the city by water. She could almost imagine herself as a mediaeval princess being ferried across the sea to meet her new husband, a wealthy Venetian merchant, mesmerised by the sight of such beautifully decorated buildings jostling shoulder to shoulder for space. Some were topped with intricate domes, others with towers pointing upwards as if in the search for space, while the water lapped at their feet. There were palaces, churches and rows of gondolas tied to candy-striped posts bobbing on the water. It was all utterly un-real. Utterly magical.

'Happy?' Raoul asked alongside her, his blue-black hair pulled into a short ponytail, his eyes covered with sun-glasses that only added to his dark appeal. Her eyes drank him in. Already he looked different, as if he'd lost some of the tension that had lined his features just yes-terday. His shirt softly draped in the breeze, sculpting against his broad chest, while the unbuttoned collar re-vealed a tantalising vee of olive skin at his neck with a sprinkling of dark hair.

A sizzling heat zipped its way up Gabriella's spine and momentarily struck her dumb. If the mediaeval prin-cess was lucky enough to have someone like this man waiting for her, she would be one very lucky woman in-deed.

But, no—this man was more likely the pirate who came to retrieve his bride from the clutches of the wealthy merchant.

He tilted his head and smiled. 'You certainly look happy.'

Happy didn't come close. She was arriving here in Venice, in a magical city with a man who took her breath away every time she looked at him. How had she ever imagined there was anything sinister about him when she had felt that sliver of apprehension yesterday in the cemetery? For his was a dark beauty that erred on the side of danger but erred deliciously, so that every glance was like a guilty pleasure to be sinfully enjoyed.

Would the fair princess stay with the rich Venetian merchant? she wondered. Or would she let herself be taken by the pirate?

No contest.

Exhilarated beyond measure, feeling suddenly more alive than she had in months, she laughed into the wind, letting the sound get taken away over the water. 'I love it. I'd forgotten how beautiful Venice is. This is just like seeing it for the first time.'

'How long has it been?'

'Years. I think I was only ten or eleven and on a school trip. I don't remember much beyond feeding the pigeons in St Mark's Square.' She shook her head, smiling as she remembered the chaos she and her class mates had caused. 'Twenty squealing girls. Those poor pigeons.'

He looked at her. 'I remember now. You told us that first night we were in the mountains while we sat around the fireplace. Everyone was laughing. I had forgotten…'

It was no wonder he had forgotten, she thought, quietly reflective for a moment. That time in the mountains had been their last holiday together. She could remember little of those first few days, either. All that stuck in her mind was the helicopter ride over the glaciers she'd been so looking forward to, and the night of illness that had put paid to any chances of her going. It was Raoul who had generously offered to stay back and look after her so their parents could go together and not miss out. Gabriella had spent the day dozing and sipping lemonade, listening to Raoul read her story after story. And they had thought nothing of it when the day had begun to darken and the night closed in. Not until the police had come calling…

'You're biting your lip again, Bella,' he said, wrapping an arm around her shoulders. 'Don't worry. We are here together now and I promise to save you from any pigeons with long-term memories.'

She laughed and turned towards him, turning away from the buildings, the water and the ladylike beauty of the city to his intensely masculine face. She was grateful that he had turned the mood around, grateful just to be here with him in this beautiful city. 'Thank you so much for allowing me to come,' she said, and reached up on tiptoes, wrapping her arms around his neck and kissing his cheek. She sighed as she relished the warm, clean scent of man, the brush of his blue-black whiskers against her lips and the feel of her body pressed length-to-length with his.

He took her arms, easing them away from his neck. She wondered if once again she had overstepped some unseen line, but he surprised her by turning her around in front of him and linking his hands at her waist where they sat, snug and disturbingly comfortable.

'We are nearly there, Bella. Look,' he said as the water taxi turned off into a smaller canal and then into another set, like a canyon amidst the tall buildings. Flowers spilled from flowerpots under arched windows; quaint bridges appeared from a wall and forded the canal, disappearing into the buildings on the other side like secret tunnels.

With Raoul's warm body at her back, his arms around her waist, she never wanted this journey to end. She was acutely aware of the constriction of his arms every time she drew breath; she was achingly aware of the proximity of them to her breasts. And then there were his hands, crossed and perched so low across her belly; she knew if he just stretched out the fingers of one hand he could touch her *there*...

It was so deliciously close it was almost impossible to breathe.

All too soon they arrived at the water door of a large *palazzo*. With a lightness that belied his size, Raoul released her and jumped to the private landing, offering his hand to help her. She looked up at the exterior of the building, drinking in the detail of walls the colour of sunset, soft blue accents around the windows and archways on the lower floor. The next boasted high-arched windows, with even a balcony complete with arched doors and marble columns. Strange; when Raoul had mentioned having an apartment in Venice, this gothic masterpiece was not what she had envisioned.

'Welcome, Raoul,' a voice said, and she looked around as an ornate arched grille swung open, revealing a man younger than Raoul by some years. 'We've been expecting you.'

'Thank you, Marco,' he said, passing him their luggage. 'This is Gabriella D'Arenberg who will be my guest for a while. Gabriella, Marco and Natania comprise my staff. I'm sure Natania will soon be along.' As he spoke, Gabriella saw a woman skip down the stairs, her layered mini skirt fluttering around her thighs. A wide smile directed at Raoul lit up her face as she appeared, her expression turning more wary when she took in their visitor. With one vertical sweep of her beautiful eyes, she gave Gabriella an inexplicable stab of jealousy. Natania was lush, gypsy-beautiful and she got to live with Raoul on a permanent basis. How on earth could he resist anything so gorgeous?

'Ah, here is Natania. Anything you need, simply ask.'

'It is a pleasure to meet you, Gabriella,' the younger man said, smiling. Gabriella could see that, while he shared Raoul's olive skin and Mediterranean colouring, that was where the similarity ended. His long, dark lashes and lush lips softened his face; even the hint of mischief in his eyes gave him a boyish charm.

'I should have warned you, we don't stand on ceremony here,' Raoul explained. 'Unless you prefer a title—miss? *Mademoiselle?*'

She shook her head. 'No, not at all. Thank you, Marco, it's lovely to meet you too.'

Natania edged closer; big hoops pierced her ears. 'It will be lovely to have another woman around for a change,' the newcomer said, holding out her slim hand, gold bangles jangling at her wrists. She moved like a colt, loose-limbed and lithe, her scooped tank top and skirt fitting smoothly, accentuating her perfect figure, the perfect complement to her wild, gypsy eyes. 'I get so bored being surrounded with just men.'

Marco jerked his head up at this, a wry grin on his lips, something heated skating over his eyes as their eyes met. Gabriella reined in that unfamiliar streak of jealousy. So Marco and Natania were a couple? That was comforting news. As was the knowledge the *palazzo* didn't see a passing parade of women.

Unjustifiable, perhaps, because what Raoul did or did not do was no real concern of hers; it wasn't as if she had any kind of stake in him. But, still, it was there and the knowledge warmed her in places still humming from his touch.

'Thank you, Natania,' she said, meaning it. 'I know I'm going to enjoy it here.'

Raoul led the way to the *piano nobile*, the noble floor, where his suite sat high above the water's edge, with views over the canal and no fear of flooding. Downstairs were the minor and service rooms, he pointed out as they climbed, while Marco and Natania shared a smaller suite of rooms on the floor above.

'You need all this space just for you?' she asked as he led her to his suite of rooms.

'Maybe not, but I won it in a card game many years ago. I was not about to quibble with the size.'

'And you kept it for an investment?'

'No. I was merely lucky enough not to lose it on the next game. Or the one after that.'

She laughed, because she could not imagine gambling with a property so clearly valuable. 'You are kidding? Surely you would not risk making the same mistake someone else had?'

'Why not? It was no risk for me because it meant nothing to me. Maybe that's why I was lucky enough to keep it. Anyway,' he said without bothering to explain as he pushed open the door to the apartment, 'Come inside.'

It wasn't a living room or even a lobby the suite opened on to, it was a library, lining four walls of the long, narrow room, bookshelves stacked high, even over doorways to the impossibly high ceilings. Gabriella did a double take, blinking with disbelief as she took in the titles, some of them recognisable treasures.

'You have a library?' she said, suddenly spinning around, a smile lighting up her face, illuminating her features with a child-like delight that twisted his gut.

So much enthusiasm.

So much life.

Such a waste.

And then she stopped spinning and stood there, almost incandescent with wonderment as she inhaled deeply, as if she could breathe in the collective wisdom contained in a room filled with old books. 'It's wonderful.'

He could not bear it. First her excitement at the *vaporetto* as they'd approached the water-borne city, an excitement that had made it impossible not to want to wrap her in his arms and feel that excitement first hand.

And now here. But this time he resisted the urge to collect her into his arms and feel first-hand the excitement in the shape of her feminine curves.

Did she always see the joy in everything?

Did she not realise it couldn't last?

'This way,' he said gruffly, almost rigid with control as he pulled open a set of double doors, unable or unwilling to stay in the room a moment longer with her. 'The living room.'

She'd done something wrong. One moment, Raoul had been warm and welcoming—even, she thought, remembering the warmth of his touch pressing against her back and the iron-like feel of his arms around her waist, more like a lover than a friend. His touch had been filled with both tenderness and desire.

Had she been the only one to feel that desire?

But now, it seemed as she watched him both physically and mentally retreat from her, there was nothing warm about him. His back was ramrod straight, the air about him frosty. Yet all she'd done was express her delight at the unexpected discovery of his library.

Had she been too easily impressed? Too gauche? Raoul was more than a decade older than her. She must seem so young and unsophisticated compared to the women he was probably used to, even if they weren't permitted here. But there would have to be women...

With a heavy heart, she followed him through the doors and into a long, richly decorated room with two long blood-red velvet sofas lining the richly frescoed walls. Four arched doors opposite led to the balcony she had seen from the sea-door landing, she assumed. But it was the chandelier that hung from the decorated ceiling that was the *pièce de résistance*. It was so exquisite that she stopped following Raoul for a moment to simply absorb its beauty. From its base swept long white plumes tipped with red, all swaying and curving, like the necks of peacocks dancing and craning their heads this way and that. The artist had captured the motion so well, it could almost have been alive.

'This is the dining room,' she heard him say. And then he must have turned, looking for her. 'It's Murano glass—an original.'

'It's exquisite,' she said, cautious, conscious of not

gushing over every last thing in case she further aggravated him.

'Have you been there? To the island, I mean, to see the glass factories?'

'Yes, my class did a tour, but I don't remember seeing anything this beautiful then.' Probably because they'd all been too fascinated with the tiny animals, the dolphins, fish and the *millefiore*—the tiny coloured flowers and hearts set in the glass—to take note of any of the more spectacular work.

'I will take you again, in that case.'

'You will?' Then she remembered not to look so excited and schooled her face into something she hoped looked far more sophisticated and calm. 'Thank you. If it's not too much trouble, that would be lovely.'

Something scudded across his eyes, and just as quickly disappeared. 'I will organise it.' Once again, he pointed to the room off one side of the living room. 'The kitchen is behind the dining room. Natania cooks most nights. And this,' he said, crossing to the other side of the living room and opening another door, 'is your room.'

She followed him into another long room, as large as the living room they had just left, with more large sofas and an amazing red Persian rug splashing colour and depth into the furnishings. But it was the king-sized bed to which her eyes were drawn. It was set into an arched alcove at the end of the room, columns at its entrance, the walls decorated with a mediaeval mural featuring nymphs and satyrs along with gods and goddesses engaged in various acts of love. It was an orgy of colour, passion and sex—the perfect lover's retreat. And he expected her to sleep there? Surrounded by that?

'Surely this is the master suite?' she said, trying not to blush and knowing she was failing miserably. She was no prude, and the art was sublime, but the images were not exactly easy to look at, not if the last thing you needed to think about was sex.

'You are my guest. And this is the most comfortable room.'

Comfortable, maybe. Confronting, *definitely*.

'There is a bathroom through here,' he said, his arm reaching for a door handle past the buttocks of a god engaged in an activity that was clearly giving him and the recipient great pleasure.

'You're blushing,' he said. 'Are you shocked by what you see?'

It wasn't that. It wasn't the sight of the images that shocked her, exactly. It was that she didn't want such thoughts put in her head when she was with Raoul. She didn't need them. It was like her every night-time dream had been captured by a mediaeval artist five-hundred years ago and had been splattered across these bedroom walls. *Raoul's bedroom walls.*

'I wasn't expecting such *unique* decor, it's true. But it's a beautiful room. In fact…' she said, fleeing for the safety of the bathroom, before realising there was no sanctuary in a place where she could just as easily imagine Raoul naked and soaping himself in the wide marble shower. She squeezed her eyes shut, trying to blot out those images too—but how did you blot out the image of a perfect male specimen, naked under the cascading water, droplets beading on the ends of his hair, rivulets sluicing down his long, hard body?

She swallowed hard and slapped on a too-bright smile as she turned. 'It's a fabulous apartment. How old is it?' As an attempt to find something safer to talk about, even if maybe it was groan-worthy, it was the best she could come up with. The fact she hadn't used the word 'naked' was something to be proud of.

'At least seven hundred years,' he said as he showed her through the rest of the apartment: the second bathroom, a small room given over to an office and a still-generous but much more modest and unassuming second bedroom. With no lovers' alcove, she noted wryly, and with which she would have been perfectly happy. 'Originally it was built on a Byzantine design, and then redesigned during the fourteenth century to what you see today.'

'It's magnificent, Raoul,' she said, no stranger to luxury herself. But there was something special about this place. It spoke of a time of both massive wealth and an unprecedented interest in the arts and all things beautiful. The *palazzo* was a temple to the beautiful, the fine, the rich and sensual.

And Raoul was like a beautiful, tortured dark angel in its midst.

'I must leave you now,' he said when they had finished the tour and he once again stood stiffly before her in the library. 'I have something I must see to. Please make yourself at home.' And then all too suddenly he was gone, leaving the air swirling in his wake.

She wandered through the apartment alone, stopping

to admire a painting or an exquisite detail on one of the many frescoes, admiring the chef's kitchen with a zillion gleaming utensils hanging from the hooks.

She stopped by the *quadrifora*, the four beautiful doors that led to the balcony, and on impulse opened them and stepped outside. A breeze tugged at her hair, and on it the scent of cooking from a *trattoria* she could see along the canal, its tables and chairs spilling out onto a terrace alongside the water. She stood there and listened to a gondolier serenade his passengers and just breathed in the scents and sounds of a city built upon the sea while her tangled thoughts lay elsewhere.

What was it that troubled Raoul? she wondered. That coloured his moods from light to dark in an instant? What was it that drove him to such dark, explosive depths, that turned his eyes unreadable and closed him off to everyone?

She stood there, long after the gondolier's song had faded along the canal, thinking about the riddle that was Raoul. Finally, finding no answers amongst the stuccoed buildings, the overflowing flowerpots or the slow, eternal slap of water against building, she sighed and thought about unpacking instead so she could go and explore.

She found Natania in her bedroom with the job already half done. 'Oh, I don't expect you to do that.'

'I don't mind. There is not enough to do otherwise, and anyway—' she lifted a cashmere sweater and rubbed it against her cheek '—you have such beautiful clothes and you wear them so well. Do you know my Marco said you looked like a flower when you arrived? Dewy and fragile and just waiting to be picked.'

Gabriella stilled as she retrieved her toilet bag from the case, heading for the bathroom. 'Marco said that?'

Natania nodded gravely, slipping tissue paper between the folds of the sweater before reverently placing it in a drawer. 'Please don't be offended. It was meant as a compliment. Only he was worried that to put you in this bedroom...' She waved a hand '...well, it might make you unsettled.'

Gabriella was still trying to work out how to answer when the other woman unzipped a compartment in her suitcase, unfolded a dress and laid it on the bed, smoothing the fabric with her hands, almost worshipping the formal gown. 'So beautiful,' she said, slipping a cover over the dress before hanging it in the closet. 'Maybe we could go shopping together while you are here?'

'I'd love to.'

The other woman's eyes lit up. 'You would? *Bene.* Anyway, I told Marco he was wrong. A woman as beautiful as you, you would know men. You would be no unpicked flower who would become unsettled by a little nudity. Am I right?'

Gabriella looked around the alcove and wondered at the other woman's definition of 'a little nudity', but she wasn't about to debate that now. For, while it was nobody's business but her own, she got the impression this was no time to act coy. She was no shy, retiring flower after all, even if she lacked the raw sensuality of this gypsy princess. 'I'm no virgin, if that's what you mean.' *Even if she could count the number of times she'd had sex on the fingers of one hand.*

The other woman's eyes opened wide, her lush mouth

in a broad self-congratulatory smile as she planted her hands on her hips and nodded. 'You see? I knew that. A woman senses these things.' She gestured to the walls around them. 'Then you will understand this art. You will appreciate it for its true beauty.' She glanced at her watch and then back at the suitcase. 'And now I must start dinner, but…'

'It's okay,' Gabriella said. 'There's not much to do. I'll finish the unpacking.'

'*Grazie!* And I promise you tonight I will make a feast fit for a king—and his queen, for that matter.' She gave an abrupt nod, as if she'd just made up her mind about something. 'Yes, it is good to see Raoul with a woman at last.'

'Natania, please don't think… It's not like that. We're old friends, that's all.'

'*Si.* Maybe for now.' And with a toss of her beautiful head she spun on her heel and headed for the kitchen, the bangles on her hand jangling in time to the sway of her hips.

What was that supposed to mean? Was Natania a fortune teller as well as a cook? But, with her spine still tingling from the gypsy's unsettling prediction, there was no way Gabriella was going to ask.

Not when she half-wished it could be true.

Raoul stormed across the square behind the *palazzo*, sending pigeons scattering while he cursed the black tide inside him that threatened to rise up, bitter and turgid, from his gut like the thick, black sludge that stuck to the piles below the water. A black tide that would not let him out of its clutches, that clogged his veins and would not let him think or act like a normal man.

He had never wanted this. He was in no position to keep anyone safe, not when he lurched from one dark mood to the next—not when he had been unable to save his own wife.

But he hated the way Gabriella had flinched back there in the library, as if he had physically lashed out and struck her—all because he was incapable of dealing with someone who saw light when he saw dark, who saw hope where there was none.

And afterwards she had withdrawn into herself, quelling her natural spirit until she had become a stilted and stunted facsimile of who she really was, and he hated himself for doing that to her even more.

If he could not repress that side of himself, he would surely frighten her away and she would never agree to marry him.

And he had promised to.

Damn himself to hell and back for it, but he had promised. What happened when you broke a promise to the dead? Did they rise up and come after you? Did they toss and turn in their graves and haunt your dreams and turn your days to nights?

He didn't want to find out. He already had enough ghosts to last a lifetime.

So he would have to woo her, court her and let her zest for life wash over him. And then afterwards, when Garbas was safely locked away behind bars and could not touch her, he would let her go.

CHAPTER FIVE

MAYBE it was Natania's cooking and the superb platter of *frittura*, the fried fish and calamari she had prepared, or maybe it was the rich *risotto al nero di seppa* made with squid ink, which Gabriella found surprisingly delicate, that served to soothe Raoul's dark mood. Or maybe it was just that his appointment had gone well. But, whatever the reason, Raoul was back to his charming best when he returned to the apartment. When he suggested an evening walking-tour of Venice after dinner, she could not resist the chance to explore the city.

The air was heavier tonight, full of humidity as a cooler change worked through, but for now it was still warm. Raoul reacquainted her with the big tourist sites, with the highly ornate Basilica di San Marco and the grand Palazzo Ducale in St Mark's Square where once long ago she'd fed and raced after pigeons with her friends. He pointed out the domed bell-tower of San Giorgio Maggiore standing on its own island across the dark slapping waters. He took her to the Rialto Bridge, the stone wonder spanning the broad Grand Canal, its central portico lit up so it looked like a grand lady dressed up for a night out. Then he showed her places that were off the main trails, wending his way through the darkening city, showing her architectural treasures and little-known pictures carved into stone walls and known only to those who knew Venice beyond the tourist routes.

He could do this, he decided as he led her to a tiny trattoria overlooking the lagoon for coffee. He could force back that black tide inside him and be civil—pleasant, even. He could be interested and attentive. And he could do this not just because he had to but because he honestly wanted to know more about her, more about those lost years when he had missed out on knowing her.

'What made you decide to become a librarian?' he asked, watching the ends of her hair play on the soft breeze as she sat down. She'd tied her hair back in a loose knot behind her head before they'd come out, but tendrils had worked their way loose and now danced around her face. He envied them their playfulness. His fingertips itched to brush them away, to linger on her soft skin…

Their coffee arrived; she thanked the waiter and looked back at him, her eyes bright and clear, smoothing the hair from her brow and tucking it behind her ears. 'I don't think there was ever a time I didn't want to do something to do with books. I actually think my profession chose me.'

He realised he liked listening to her too. He liked the sound of her accent, the blend of half-French, half-English, the best of both, Cognac over cream.

'Tell me what you love about it,' he urged.

'It's just working with books, all of them, every one

of them an entire world between the covers. Every new one is a discovery and until you dip into them you just never know what's inside: new worlds; new discoveries; new characters who leap off the page. It's all there, just waiting for you to open the cover and turn the page.'

She was so bright, so passionate, and even while he felt the darkness rise, even as his gut churned and rebelled, still it was impossible not to feel that light shine out from her and warm him in places where light had not touched for so long.

'The books in my library,' he bit out, coming up with an idea that might hold her, something to keep her interest while she stayed. 'I don't even know what's there.'

He watched her brow pucker as she sensed the almost-crime. 'Maybe while I'm here—if you didn't mind, that is—maybe I could look at them and catalogue them for you.'

'You would do that for me?'

'I would love to.'

She was so excited, he believed she would.

'What about you?' she asked as he finished his coffee, so suddenly that he was taken by surprise.

'What about me?'

'What have you been doing all these years?'

Standing still.

Trying to forget.

'Nothing half as interesting as you.'

She tilted her head. 'I was sorry to hear that your wife died. You were married such a short time.'

The black tide grew closer. 'What did you hear?'

'Only that there was some kind of tragic accident.

But it's such a long time ago now. Did you never think of remarrying?'

Never.

He pushed his chair back. 'Why don't we walk?'

A mist had grown while they'd sat in the café, rolling in over the sea, devouring everything in its path. Gabriella forgot about her question and thought there was something so utterly fascinating and serene about watching an entire world slowly vanish, a fantasy world disappearing into the fog as if it had never been real, as if it had never existed.

They found a bridge looking out over the water where the deepening mist rolled in over the lagoon, obliterating and absorbing everything, even sounds, so that it was as though Venice had been buried under a dank, white cloud. Every now and then a light would appear, or the dull rumble of an engine would herald the ghostly shape of a vessel making its way back to shore. She shivered. 'Are you cold?' he asked, putting his arm around her shoulders.

'It's spooky,' she said, looking up at him. 'Don't you feel it?'

He looked out into the mist-covered lagoon and she wondered what he was looking for when all anyone could see was white. 'The ghosts come out,' he said, 'When there is a night like this.'

'Oh, Raoul, please,' she said, trying to laugh while she fought down the prickles rising at the back of her neck and the shivers running down her spine. 'I'm not a child you can frighten so easily.'

'No, it is true. There are many, many ghosts in Venice. And many, many stories.'

And, because she had told him she was no longer a child and could not be frightened so easily, she felt she had no choice but to boldly ask, 'Like what? Tell me one of your ghost stories, then.'

Still looking out in the mist, a look so intense it was almost enough to make her regret her rash challenge, he began, his voice low and heavy with foreboding. 'Once there was a wealthy merchant who had the world at his feet. He had riches beyond measure—he was good-looking, some even said—and he had a beautiful wife, famous and talented. And he thought that he had it all. He thought that he was happy.'

She held her breath as the fog swirled silently around them, knowing this could not end well.

'And then one night, a night filled with the pleasures of the flesh as so much of his life had become, he introduced his wife to two brothers, supposedly two friends of his. But the two brothers conspired against him. They promised the merchant's wife the world and spirited her away.'

'She went willingly?'

He shrugged. 'Who can say? The man was a fool, you see, who saw nothing before him but his perfect life, and nothing afterwards but a blind rage. And when he found her one storm-ridden night, lying with one of the brothers, it almost destroyed him.'

'What happened?'

'They died that night, both the woman and her lover.'

'The merchant killed them?'

'He might as well have. Because she haunted him every night afterwards until he thought he was going mad with the darkness. And even now, on nights such as these, you can hear her voice on the mournful breeze calling for him, searching for him, waiting for him to pass by so she can suck him into the watery depths.'

Through the gloom of the fog the soft wind moaned and a light flickered faintly once, twice, before it disappeared back into the swirling fog. Gabriella grabbed hold of Raoul's arm, chilled beyond measure. 'It's late,' she said, trying not to tremble as she clung to him. 'And it's been a long day. Let's go home.'

They walked back hand in hand, the soft lamps along their route and Raoul's solid presence banishing thoughts of ghosts, legends and what must have been just wild imaginings, turning her thoughts away from the ghostly and much more towards the physical and the real. Her hand fitted well in his, she mused; his long fingers were warm and strong. She squeezed her hand and he squeezed back, looking down at her. 'I want you to be happy, Bella. Are you glad you came to Venice?'

She smiled, thinking she would be happy to be with Raoul anywhere when he was like this—charming, warm and the perfect host. But to be here with him in Venice, against the backdrop of mediaeval *palazzos*, with the rumble of the *vaporettos* and the snatches of love songs from passing gondoliers, she couldn't think of a better place to be. 'It's magical, Raoul. Thank you for insisting I come.'

He stopped and pulled her to him, his free hand curving around her neck and sending delicious shivers cours-

ing through her as leaned down, his eyes on her mouth.
She gasped as their lips met, breathing in the taste of
him, dark, rich and potent, much like the man himself.
His mouth weaved some kind of magic on hers. So ten-
der and evocative was his kiss that she wanted to fall into
it and go with it wherever it might lead so that, when he
lifted his head, she almost mewled a protest.

'What was that for?' she asked, suddenly breathless
and dizzy, hoping for all kinds of things that were probably as unlikely as building an entire city on water—yet
here it was.

'Because,' he said, his dark eyes swirling with heated
intent, 'There was no way earthly way I could not.'

She lay awake a long time that night in the big king-sized
bed surrounded by the endless orgy, a celebration of the
act of love in all its iterations, still reeling from Raoul's
kiss, still tingling at the memory of his touch and the
sensual brush of his lips against her own.

Buzzing at the erotic images on the walls around her.

On the wall before her a nymph kissed her lover, his
hand at her plump breast. She could almost imagine that
hand on hers, tweaking her nipple, coaxing it to hardness. With a groan she turned over, willing herself to
think of something less sensual, less arousing—only to
be welcomed by a wild-eyed woman, her head thrown
back in ecstasy as her lover pressed close behind her.
She turned on her stomach, buried her face in the pillow and tried to ignore the ache in her breasts and the
pulsing insistence between her thighs.

Such a big bed.

Such a lonely bed.

Such a waste.

And when she did fall asleep it was to restless dreams of potent, well-built gods, wicked satyrs—and a dark and dangerous man who kissed like one of those gods, who probably made love like one of those gods and who was sleeping a mere room away...

Raoul was out when she rose the next day, so she pulled on jeans and sneakers and a singlet top that could afford to get dusty and threw herself into the task of cataloguing the library while he was away. Marco found her a step ladder so she could reach all but the highest shelves and promised he would help her when she got to those. Even on the lower shelves, the breadth of the collection dazzled her. Mostly they were books printed in Italian, as she had expected, but a quick scan revealed titles on geography, the sciences, history and the arts, with some dusty tomes at least a century old; a veritable treasure trove.

She flipped through one volume, a history of the *palazzos* of Venice by the looks of it, its spine creaking with age and stiffness. But the illustrations were still wonderful, leaping from the page with life, the buildings along the Grand Canal instantly recognisable even now. Her heart raced with the possibilities of her task—maybe there were volumes here that had never been documented before. Why not?

But with only her schoolgirl Italian to help her she would need help. One of her colleagues from the library would be able to help her, she was sure. She needed to call her boss anyway. She would call later today, when she had more idea of the size of the task ahead.

Then with a pang she remembered she needed to find out what was happening with Consuelo. She had barely spared him a thought ever since she'd arrived, yet there must be news by now. Even if he could not answer her messages, someone must know what was happening to him. Raoul had intimated there was nothing she could do, but there had to be something she could do to help. She was a friend, after all, and he would do the same for her; she was sure of it.

She was just about to descend the ladder when she saw it—the slim volume wedged tightly between two others. Even with her imperfect Italian she could make out the title: *Ghostly Tales of Venice*.

Thinking it must have been the source of Raoul's story, she pulled it out, curious, leafing through the pages and searching for his story of the wealthy merchant who was haunted by his lost love. She flipped the pages, just able to decipher a few words here and there. One was a story of children lost in the mist who had disappeared for ever, their gondola found floating listlessly the next day. Another was of a murdered soul who haunted the bridge where he was brutally killed, and yet another told of a woman lost at sea whose unearthly casket could be seen floating on the lagoon on mist-shrouded nights.

Maybe Raoul had been right, she thought as she flipped through the book, her blood running cold with even just a snatched word here and there and a pencil-sketch illustration. Maybe there really were ghosts in

Venice's mist-shrouded waterways. She had felt something last night; she was sure of it.

But she reached the last page of the slim volume and closed the book without finding what she had been looking for. There was no mention of Raoul's wealthy merchant, nothing that came close to the story he had told her, of the wife lost with her lover who had haunted her merchant husband ever since.

And like the cold slice of steel through flesh an idea came to her and she wondered...

Had it been a legend?

Or had Raoul been telling his very own ghost story?

The lost wife, the tragic death, the darkness he seemed to carry around with him as if the past still had hold of him, weighing him down, refusing to let him go. Was Raoul that haunted merchant?

She clutched the small book to her chest and shivered as she remembered the cool detachment with which he had related the tale, as if it had had nothing to do with him. But Raoul too had lost his wife in tragic circumstances. And he had cut Gabriella off earlier when she had expressed her sympathy, changing the subject. Had the story been his way of explaining something he found too difficult to talk about?

Her heart went out to him. Hadn't they both suffered enough when they had lost their parents? Yet Raoul had suffered another blow by losing his wife not long after.

She started down the ladder, the book still clutched in her hand. It was so unfair.

It would be enough to drive any man to despair.

She resolved that she would not cause him more pain.

As he had come to her rescue with Umberto's death, rescuing her from her sudden loneliness, so she too would do everything she could to ease his suffering so that he would never rue the day he had invited her here.

She was almost at the last step when the door swung open behind her. One-handed, she turned and lost her footing, and would have fallen, but he was there to steady her, his hand like a steel clamp around her wrist, the other at her waist, easing her gently down to the floor. 'Bella, what are you doing?'

She looked up at him, breathless and grateful, intending to find him a sympathetic smile, to let him know she understood about his pain and his loss. But just the very sight of him warmed her soul so much—his dark features, the angles, planes and dark recesses that combined to stir her senses—that her smile became so much more besides. 'Raoul,' she said as he bent down to kiss her cheeks, leaving her almost breathless as his evocative scent filled her lungs. 'I thought I would get started on your library. To earn my keep.'

'I have a better way,' he suggested. 'It is a beautiful day outside. Come and share it with me.'

'But the library?'

'Has waited this long. It will still be there tomorrow. Come, Bella—you *do* want to see something of Venice while you are here?'

'Of course. I'll just go and get changed.'

'Please don't,' he said, his voice tight. 'You look good in anything you wear—but in those jeans, Bella...' And his words put a sizzle all the way to her bones. Then he tilted his head and looked almost genuinely contrite.

'I probably should not say such things.'

'It's okay,' she said, licking suddenly dry lips—the dust from the books, she assumed. 'I don't mind. I... I'll just grab my jacket.'

He had her. From the moment he had kissed her on that Venice path last night, he had sensed that she was his. Ridiculously easily, as it happened. He could not imagine why any woman, let alone one as beautiful and filled with life as Gabriella, would be drawn to someone as dark and as accursed as him. But for whatever reason—maybe that trait in her that had her believing the best in everyone—she seemed all too ready to forgive him his faults, if he could only repress that dark part of him and act civilised every now and then.

So he donned the air of a civilised man, not one plagued by dark deeds and darker moods. In the ensuing days, he showed her the best of Venice. He walked her to the Castello area in the evening, lingering in the Giardini—the gardens created only two short centuries ago after Napoleon's invasion—then spent time in the Via Garibaldi, where they sipped bitter spritz with fat green olives amongst the locals taking time out. He took her to the museums and galleries, both the well-known and obscure, and he treated her to the best and least well-known of Venice's restaurants on the outlying islands, while treating her to the most exclusive of Venice's boutiques nearby.

He listened to her talk, seemingly endlessly, about the books she'd discovered in his library where she explored every day. And he let her joy of discovery wash over him, knowing he must if she was to trust him.

He had been the perfect host. And tonight would be no exception, he decided as he slipped on his jacket. Tomorrow he would take her to the glass-making factories and shops of Murano, but tonight would provide one more piece for the fairy-tale picture she was building up of Venice. And, if tonight's excursion went as well as expected, they would be shopping tomorrow for more than just glass.

He swallowed back on the now-familiar pang of guilt, that what he was doing might be wrong or unfair, or was somehow taking advantage of her. Because it wasn't as if he didn't like her. It wasn't as if he had to pretend to be attracted to her; it wasn't as if he had to lie about those things. They were old friends, he told himself, and it wasn't as though he planned to hurt her. He was protecting her, just as her grandfather had requested.

And Umberto had been right—there would be nothing worse for her than if she fell into the clutches of someone like Garbas.

If marrying her was what it took to prevent that, he would do it.

Gabriella's body hummed with anticipation as she waited. Raoul had promised her something special tonight, a secret he had refused to reveal, even when she had teased him and begged him to let her in on the secret.

He was different, she decided as she looked down from the balcony at the never-dull vista that greeted her. Could one ever get sick of the sight and sounds of Venice? It was a world unto itself—a place of incredible beauty on the one hand, of secrets and hidden depths on the other.

Just like Raoul himself.

For even lately in these last few days, even when he had played the host role to perfection, there had been times—glimpses, really—when she would turn her head and look at him, catch him unawares and see *something* lurking in the depths. Something troubled, menacing and sometimes even sinister that made her want to reach out with her hands, smooth his brow, untangle his thoughts—and then he would look up, see her watching him and smile, chasing the shadows away.

Venice suited him, she thought, sighing into the soft breeze and, just like Venice, he was unique. One of a kind. Impossible not to fall in love with.

She stilled at the railing, her heart skipping a beat and then resuming just that slight bit quicker. She couldn't love him, could she? Not really?

Sure, she had always loved him; he had been almost family.

Except that wasn't what she was thinking now.

When she had been no more than a child, she had worshipped him as a child worshipped someone she adored like a hero, someone she could look up to.

As an adolescent, her fantasies had been based more on fairy tales and rampant teenage hormones, of a fantasy Raoul that was larger than life that she could only dream about, the product of her own wild imagination.

And now?

Now she was a woman. Surely she did not imagine

that tingle every time they touched? Surely she did not imagine the magic of their kiss?

Those things were no fantasy.

Those things were real.

But love? Could she really be falling in love with Raoul? They had been together just a few short days, after all.

She must be crazy even to think it.

She must be.

And yet the magic of the last few days had not simply been all about Venice. Venice delighted her, it was true. But it wasn't Venice that had her blood pounding or her heartbeat quickening right now, it was the thought of spending the evening with Raoul. Of losing herself in his bottomless gaze and feeling the heat from his body feed into hers, warming her in an endless, sensual glow.

It was more than just Venice.

It was Raoul, and she was falling in love with him.

He found her waiting for him in the living room, standing on the balcony overlooking the canal, her expression pensive. She was more beautiful than ever in a soft pastel-print dress with a cinched waist and full skirt that made the most of her tan skin, chestnut hair and the near-sinful proportions of her figure, the feminine curve from breast through waist to hip.

When had he gone from merely noticing that she had grown up to thinking she had grown into a very desirable woman? When had just a glance at her turned from benevolent approval of the changes time had brought about to something deeper and more fundamental, something that stirred his blood and sent it simmering? Right now, it seemed like he had wanted her for ever.

She turned when she heard him approach, her smile wide, welcoming and totally innocent—and that pang of guilt made itself known again, twisting this time, mercilessly so. He wished there was something about her he did not like, something he could find fault with aside from her unswerving faith in her human companions.

Except that it was that very fault—the trait that made her see the best in the likes of that scum Garbas—that was also making his job so very, very easy.

'Are you ready, Bella?' he said, taking her hands in his. 'For tonight's adventure?'

Her eyes held so many stars he could not count; her eager smile was infectious and he laughed in spite of his own misgivings and his own endless doubts. 'Then let's go.'

Tonight the air was warm and blessed with only the lightest of breezes, the architecture of Venice turning honey gold under the westering sun.

'This evening,' he said as he handed her into the gondola waiting at the sea door, 'We continue our exploration of Venice from the water.'

Together they sat back on the plushly cushioned reclining seat as the gondolier let the vessel drift away, setting it moving along the canal with long, languid sweeps through the water.

They ventured into the Grand Canal, past St Mark's Square, still heaving with tourists and its cloud of pigeons, past all of the sights that Raoul had shown her on foot. Only this way showed Venice as it was always meant to be seen—from the sea, where the water offered an unbeatable perspective of the wonders that rose all around them.

He had judged his timing well. Gabriella sat entranced, reclining in the curve of his arm, as comfortably wound against him as a cat, and he sensed that if he asked her this day to fly to the moon she would say yes.

Right on cue, the rich tenor voice of their gondolier rang out in the balmy evening air.

'Raoul,' she said, her eyes so bright and brilliant they threatened to rival the moon's pearlescent glow. 'Did you plan this?'

He drew her closer to him and smoothed a loose tendril of her hair with his hand. 'Are you happy, Bella?'

'I don't think I have ever been happier.' And she settled deeper, curving her delicious body against him, making him burn. Tonight, he thought, she was his. All he had to do was ask the question.

The gondola slipped along the canals, gently slicing through the water, taking the route Raoul had instructed the gondolier to take, getting closer and closer to that moment—and to the task he had promised himself he would undertake tonight.

Except, the further the boat ventured, the heavier and darker his gut felt. How was he supposed to keep her safe? What if he couldn't? What if he failed again? For she was beautiful, too beautiful for him. Too beautiful to be shackled to a man with a dark past and no future, even if he told himself it need only be for a few months, just until he knew she was free from Garbas. Too beautiful to be shackled to a man who could not keep anyone safe, not even his own wife.

'It's a beautiful night,' she said, nestling closer to him. 'At least we will be safe from your ghosts tonight.'

He stilled, for there were always ghosts. She had been gone ten years and still she would not let him go.

She would never let him go.

He felt Gabriella shift against him, protesting his sudden stiffness. 'Raoul, is something wrong?'

'I'm sorry, Bella,' he said, trying to force himself to relax. Tonight was no time to remember, to think of ghosts, horrors and mistakes that belonged in the past. Tonight there was a job to be done. 'Look,' he continued, pointing ahead, wanting to change the subject for his own sake as much as to distract her. 'The Bridge of Sighs.'

Before them the white limestone bridge arched gracefully over the Rio di Palazzo, connecting the old prison to the interrogation rooms in the Doge's Palace. 'I read about that,' she said. 'And how Lord Byron gave it that name for the prisoners who would sigh as they took their last view of the city from the windows of the bridge before being taken away to meet their fate.'

He nodded, feeling an uncomfortable tightness constrict his chest. 'That is indeed one story of the bridge,' he managed, his heart beating faster, his blood pumping louder in his ears as the moment he had been planning drew nearer. 'There is another—much more romantic, as it happens. They say that if lovers kiss at sunset under the Bridge of Sighs they will find blissful happiness with each other for the rest of their lives.'

The boat glided along the canal, its companions the gentle slap and whisper of water and the gondolier's evocative serenade. He looked down at her where he cradled her in his arms, her face close to his, the slanting rays of sunlight warming her brandy-coloured eyes, eyes filled to the brim with expectation as she waited for his kiss.

This was it.

It was time.

CHAPTER SIX

RAOUL looked down into her eyes. Neither the darkness of his past nor the ghosts that plagued him were enough to stop him now.

And, even though he knew it was insane, that he was the last person to deserve her, he wanted her—wanted all of her, at least for tonight. For the promise he had made, he told himself. Only so she might believe it to be true.

The setting sun turned the air molten around them, shimmering with a thousand wishes, a thousand hopes. The first of his wants, he knew was in his control. His lips brushed hers as he sensed the shadow of the bridge move over them while his lips tasted, explored, tested.

Her mouth melded to his willingly as she gave herself up to his kiss, her sweet, sweet lips parting in invitation, an invitation he had no power but to accept as he felt the heat in his body build as her body curled into him, her hot mouth dragging him in.

And it was his turn to go willingly, losing himself in her liquid depths, plundering her mouth, wanting to reach deeper, harder. Needing more.

Their kiss started at the Bridge of Sighs, but it did

not end there. It did not end anywhere close to there. For
the first time in her life, she felt truly alive, every part
of her tingling with hot awareness, as if a switch had
been thrown and her body was humming with electric-
ity looking for somewhere to go. Looking for release of
a charge that would burn her up if she couldn't let go.

Until all too soon they were back at the *palazzo*.

'We are home,' Raoul whispered against her sensitive lips, tracing the pad of one finger down her cheek.
'It is time to go.'

'Already?' she asked, too comfortable to move, and
he chuckled softly, a satisfying, rumbling sound that
said he wasn't done with her yet either.

'It does not have to be the end...'

She blinked up at him, sensing the invitation in his
words, giving her the choice when there was really no
choice at all. 'Make love with me, Raoul.'

This time he didn't chuckle. Instead he growled and
scooped her up into his arms, not letting the sudden sway
of the vessel throw him from his stride as he lifted her
bodily from the gondola and through the sea door, his
lips once more meshed with hers as he negotiated the
route up the stairs and into the apartment.

He found her room, lit in the soft night glow of the
city, hesitating momentarily before laying her almost
reverently on the wide bed. For the first time she didn't
see the endless orgy going on around her, didn't envy
them, because Raoul was here with her and soon she
would be his.

He growled again as he joined her, collecting her into
his arms as he pulled her into his kiss.

She was drowning, she decided. She had been drowning all night, finding it impossible to draw air, finding it impossible to breathe or to think or to anything but drown under a torrent of sensation.

And drowning had never felt so good.

His hot mouth was at her throat, his hands moulding her to him, length to delicious length, joining them at breast and thigh and making her gasp when she felt him against her belly, hard, insistent and wanting.

What little air there had been was consumed in a raging heat that started and ended between her thighs.

Her hands tangled in his hair, urgent and busy, sliding the tie from its length. Her fingers luxuriated in its silky weight as he dipped his head and took her breast in his mouth. Even fully clothed she felt his hot breath sear her skin, felt his teeth graze one sensitive nipple until she cried out with the pleasure of sensation and the frustration of the barrier of clothing.

He was already ahead of her, his long fingers working at the buttons of her blouse, peeling it away, dispensing too with her skirt and sliding it down her legs, unwrapping her, opening her up to his gaze. She waited, afraid and tremulous, unable to breathe while he lifted his head, wanting him to like what he saw, needing both his approval and his desire.

In a face built of shadows and darkness, his eyes gleamed in the soft slanting light as his hands traced their way back up her legs, resting flat-palmed on her belly, his fingertips tracing the line of her lace bra. 'Bella,' he said. His voice was so low and filled with gravel that it seemed she felt his words through the touch of his fingers rather than heard him speak. 'You are so perfect.' He dragged in air, his dark eyes looking suddenly tortured, confused. 'But I… Bella, I do not deserve…'

'I want you,' she said, empowered by the raw admiration she had seen in his eyes, the raw power before whatever doubts had crept into his mind, about whatever sense of wrong he was committing. This was not wrong and it never could be. She raised herself onto one elbow, unclipping her bra with her free hand, coaxing the strap down her arm, letting the scrap of lace fall from her breasts. 'I want you to make love to me, Raoul. I want to feel you deep inside me.'

He groaned then, a sound that seemed rent from his very soul. It was so very dark and anguished that for a moment she was afraid he might leave her—but then he looked at her, his chest heaving, and his eyes told her he was going nowhere. His fingers worked at his shirt, reefing it off, and she could not resist putting her hand to his skin, drinking in the complexities of his skinscape—the sculpted flesh, the wiry brush of hair, the nuggety nub of a nipple.

He hissed in air when she flicked that nub with the nail of her thumb, already shrugging down his trousers, kicking off his shoes, brushing off his underwear with the sweep of one hand that exposed all of him to her gaze.

She gasped at his size, her body sizzling at the raw, masculine potency, and she saw his eyes glint at her reaction before he tumbled her back on the bed.

'You're beautiful,' she said, awed by the power and

beauty of his body under her hands as he rained kisses on her skin, her throat, her belly, her breasts, making her cry out as he rolled his tongue around one sensitive nipple, drawing it into his hot, liquid mouth.

All the time the need inside her coiled tighter and more insistent, so that when his hand scooped down her side and brushed her last scrap of clothing she thought she might explode.

'Raoul!' she cried. He shushed her with his kiss, tangling his tongue with hers, pulling her deeper as his fingers slipped under the lace and through her neat curls, parting her with just the tip of one incendiary finger. Never had she felt like this, breathless, overwhelmed and on the cusp of something so magnificent, so momentous. Never had she felt so out of control.

'I need you,' she said—yet Raoul showed no mercy, drawing her nipple into his mouth, sliding his fingers deeper into her hot, slick darkness, his thumb circling that exquisitely sensitive nub, where it seemed all her nerve endings coalesced, one finger pushing inside her, almost sending her over the edge.

Her hands flailed on the bed, searching for something—anything. She found him, rock-hard, hot and already beading with moisture, and it was his turn to groan as he pulsed and bucked in her hand.

'Bella,' he said, grinding the word out between his teeth as though she was hurting him.

'I want you,' she repeated, writhing under him, knowing that if he didn't make love to her right now she would surely burn up in these desperate, all-consuming flames. 'Please, I need you!'

This time he showed blessed mercy, whisking off her remaining garment with an efficiency she might have congratulated in other, less urgent circumstances but right now any delay was too long, any time a waste, when all she wanted in the entire world was to be joined with this man.

Then he was back and she mewled with pleasure and surprise to realise one of them had been aware enough to think of protection as she pulled him into her kiss. He eased her legs apart, his clever fingers returning to once again caress, tease and drive her wild with need until she could not bear it a moment longer.

She tilted her hips in invitation, thrashing her head from side to side, driven crazy with longing, need and something like insanity. Just when she could not stand it any more, he was there at her entrance, and everything in her body seemed to concentrate and focus down on that one, tenuous, madness-inducing contact; that one hitched moment in time where the whole world—the satyrs, sirens, gods and goddesses—all waited with bated breath.

And then he entered her, filling her with one long thrust that drove her head back into the pillows and the breath from her lungs as her body stretched to accommodate his fullness.

Nothing, nothing in the world—not the first sun of spring on her skin, the fresh whisper of breeze through her hair after a long summer day or even seeing Raoul appear through the swirling mists that day—had ever felt so good.

Until he shifted inside her and the best got better.

Her eyes found focus, found his dark eyes watching her as he slowly withdrew and waited on the brink only to fill her even deeper, so that she gasped. But she kept her eyes on his, even as the storm inside her built with every slow withdrawal, with every sliding thrust; even as the rhythm between their bodies built, even as the pace became frantic and their breath with it, even as sensation coiled, intensified, built and built.

Built until there was no place higher to build, no place yet to go. With one final, urgent thrust, one cry of triumph, he made the stars and moon collide and sent their tiny sparkling shards raining down all around her, spelling out the words she already knew to be true.

I love you, Raoul.

It wasn't supposed to be like this. He collapsed alongside her, dragging in air as if his life depended on it, wondering what the hell had just happened. Make love to her, he had thought. Seduce her. That was what he had planned.

So why did he feel like he was the one who had been seduced? Why did he feel like he had been the one handed a precious gift?

She had told him that she wanted him.

She had told him that she wanted to feel him deep inside.

She had wrapped those hot fingers around him and brought him to the very edge of his control.

And, in the sex-fogged recesses of his mind, he knew only one thing: that, for both their sakes, this marriage could not come soon enough.

* * *

The call came the next morning. He should have slept, and slept late, given the night of love-making they had had, but Raoul had slipped out of her bed early, unable to rest under the lover's alcove. He had been feeling claustrophobic, hemmed in by the audience, mocked by the smiling satyrs and pitied by their lovers, as if they knew the truth.

So when the call had come he had been there to take it—to hear the news that Garbas, courtesy of the finest criminal lawyers in Europe, had been granted bail against all odds. Worse still, word from the street was that one of the first places he had visited on his release was Gabriella's home, looking for her. No doubt needing access to her wealth to fund his defence.

So he had been right to bring her to Venice with him, he acknowledged as he terminated the call. Now he just needed to finish the job he had set himself.

With Garbas on the loose, he would have to do something sooner rather than later—otherwise he would soon track Gabriella down, discover she was in Venice and try to play the friendship card. He could not let that happen.

He glanced at his watch and then back towards the bedroom where Gabriella still lay sleeping and probably would for hours. Half of him yearned to rejoin her in bed, to be there when she woke up, make love to her warm, willing body and blot everything out—the deathbed promise, the past, Garbas. Blot it all out with the glories of her body and the passion of their love-making.

But he could not afford to think that way. Making love

to her was a means to an end, nothing more. He could not afford to let it be more.

So he would leave for Paris now, talk to his contacts and find out what had gone wrong with the police case. And meanwhile Natania could take Gabriella on the promised trip to Murano.

She might be disappointed he would not be taking her, but he would make up for it tonight.

'I don't know whether to stay in Venice or go home.'

On the other end of the call, Gabriella heard Phillipa's soft expression of concern. 'Do you really have a choice?'

That was exactly Gabriella's problem—she didn't know. She'd woken deliciously warm cocooned in the bed clothes, wondering if last night's love-making had been a dream, being told by the protest and creak of unfamilar muscles that it was not. She'd woken with a smile on her face and with joy in her heart.

And if Raoul had been there to hold her close and make love to her again there would have been no question in her mind. There was no place she would rather be.

But she had woken up after the most wondrous night of her life *alone*.

And Natania's explanation that Raoul had apologised but had promised to be back in time for dinner went no way to diminishing this overwhelming sense of abandonment.

Hadn't last night meant anything to him? All night his body had told her he loved her. All night she'd waited for him to say the words, expecting him to say the words she had found herself so close to saying every time she looked at him.

Yet this morning he had gone without a word.

'I don't know,' she said, shaking her head, trying to clear her muddied thoughts. 'I guess I really should go home and sort out the estate some time, and then I have to do something about returning to work. And Consuelo finally texted this morning and wants to catch up...' Then she thought about leaving Raoul, the man who had blown her world apart. 'But...'

'But what? Is it Raoul?'

'He makes me feel so good, Phillipa. He makes me feel so alive.'

'Ah.' There was a pause. 'Do you love him?'

Gabriella breathed out in a rush, 'I think so.'

'And does Raoul feel the same way about you?'

That was where Gabriella came unstuck. What did a man feel for you, if he could make love to you all night and then disappear with the morning without so much as a sweet kiss to remember him by—a man who told you nothing of how he felt?

Unless he was deliberately trying to give her the message that their love-making didn't mean anything. But that made no sense when she thought of how he had almost worshipped her body. Surely he could not be that callous?

'I don't know, Phillipa. It's driving me crazy, but I just don't know.'

'Then it's easy, Gabriella. Everything has happened so quickly, it's no wonder you're confused. So, go home. Sort out the estate, go back to work and catch up with

Consuelo if you must. But just take some time to clear your head. And, if he's the one for you, if he truly loves you, you will know.'

'How will I know?'

'Because he won't be able to live without you.'

When Phillipa put it like that, it all made such sense. She was too close to him here, in this fantasy *palazzo* in one of the most romantic cities in the world, it was no wonder she couldn't think straight.

She would tell him tonight at dinner.

The decision made, her flight home booked for the next day, Gabriella spent the afternoon with Natania. They wandered the fascinating shops and factories of Murano, shop after shop filled with the beautiful, the most stunning and even the most whimsical expressions of the glass-makers' art in colours of brilliant blues and reds, some laced with gold.

Cabinet after cabinet was filled with intricate bottles, glasses and ornaments, while chandeliers, hung from every ceiling ranging from the traditional to the ultra-modern.

The two women prowled the shops, stopping here and there to admire something beautiful, Gabriella found herself enjoying the day out much more than she had expected, maybe because she'd made her decision and it felt like she was taking back control of her life; maybe because Natania was such good company. One of her cousins worked on the island and her knowledge of the various glass-making techniques and styles was better than any guided tour.

Gabriella took the opportunity to buy an intricate perfume-bottle for Phillipa. And, while Natania was busy talking to her cousin, purchased a necklace that simply begged to be around Natania's neck—a glass heart, a brilliant red with splashes of gold, wild and sensual like the woman herself. It would be her thank-you gift.

She was just paying for her purchases when Natania said farewell to her cousin and they moved onto the next store—the last one, she had promised herself, before they caught the water taxi home so she could pack.

'Why must you leave so soon?' asked Natania beside her.

'I can hardly stay here for ever. I have a job I have to get back to in Paris some time. And a house waiting that is being neglected in my absence. Plus, there are the friends I want to visit.'

Natania nodded to her long list of reasons and asked, 'So, do you love him?'

Gabriella simply blinked. Natania was the second person to ask that question today. Was it so obvious? She sighed, conceding the point, knowing there was no point beating around the bush with her. 'I think I have always loved him, Natania—as a friend. But lately, that love has changed…'

The other woman nodded, as if satisfied. 'He is not an easy man to love. He has a dark past that colours his world.' Almost immediately she moved away to investigate another table of ornaments. Gabriella followed, intrigued. 'How long exactly have you worked for Raoul?'

She shrugged, setting the gold hoops in her ears bouncing while her eyes searched the past. 'Ten years, maybe eleven. I am not so good with numbers.'

'Did you ever meet his wife?'

She threw a glance over her shoulder. 'That was not a good time for him.'

'So you met her?'

'No. But I saw what it did to him. I saw what it cost. It was an ugly time.'

Gabriella wanted to ask why, and what else she wasn't telling her, except then she found it—what she had been looking for all the time she had been on Murano and hadn't even realised.

A gift for Raoul.

It was sitting amidst a sea of pretty ornaments, so many, too many to choose from, but this one was different. This one spoke to her. A paperweight. And at its base it swirled with darkness, clouds of purple to black, like the dark, dank sea. As it rose, the colours shifted and turned, still complex and rich in density but with the promise of light captured in the darkness. At the very top it was the clearest, sparkling crystal while at its heart sat a brilliant splash of red.

It was Raoul, she realised as she picked it up and held it in her hand. It was Raoul and all his complexities, all his moods. And his heart, locked away somewhere deep inside it all, the heart he had shown her these last few days—the heart he had all but given her last night.

Maybe she would leave and he would not follow her, be able to live without her—but she could leave him with this, and maybe one day he would understand.

CHAPTER SEVEN

GABRIELLA found him in his office, already back from Paris on their return. 'Raoul?' He turned at her voice. 'Am I interrupting? Is this a bad time?'

'No, of course not,' he said, closing down his laptop. 'Come in.' He rose to meet her, kissing her cheeks, warming her senses with his signature scent, bringing back last night's memories in a rush that had her cheeks flushing and her body preparing all over again for their coupling. 'You are a sight for sore eyes, Bella. I'm sorry I could not have been with you today.'

'It doesn't matter,' she said, only a half lie. While it had mattered at the time, now it merely increased her resolve that what she was doing was right. Time and distance were what she needed, despite what her body kept trying to tell her. 'How did your business go?'

He waved his hand as if dismissing it. 'A nuisance, nothing more, but unfortunately it had to be dealt with today.' He took her hand. 'I hated to leave you like I did but I was loath to wake you, knowing how little sleep you got. Can you forgive me?'

She tried to ignore the flush of heat that flowed into her arm at his touch but there was no ignoring the heat that infused her face. They both knew he was the reason she'd had so little sleep. 'I found you a present,' she said, wanting to change the subject before she thought about what he could do to her to earn her forgiveness. 'While we were in Murano.'

He stilled, sensing something was not quite right. She was nervous and distant, as though she'd erected a wall between them in the hours since he'd left her sleeping. He cursed the impulse that had seen him take off for Paris rather than handle what was happening here. But then, something had changed last night, something that he had not planned, and he had needed the space to deal with it.

'You do not need to buy me gifts,' he said. *You would not want to, if you only knew...*

'It's nothing. Here,' she said, holding out the package to him.

He regarded it solemnly before taking the surprisingly heavy gift, strangely touched by this unexpected gesture.

'Open it,' she urged. Once again he caught a glimpse of that enthusiasm she had, that bright spark of life he'd once found so challenging, a quality he now associated with her and that he looked for—because it would mean his dark heart had not extinguished that spark, despite his early moodiness. 'Unless,' she added, a little sadly, he thought, 'You would rather open it later?'

'No,' he said with a shake of his head, not wanting her to be sad now, knowing that there was enough disappointment and sadness ahead of her. Cursing himself, because with Garbas free he could see no way around it. 'I want to see what you have found me.'

So he slipped off the ribbon and peeled open the tissue paper until he held the cool, glass weight of her gift in the palm of his hand.

'It's a paperweight,' she said unnecessarily. 'I thought you could use it in your office. It reminded me of you.'

He lifted it to the light, examining the mix of dark and light, the skilful melding and weaving of the different levels of colour with a core of intense red at its centre. With an electric charge up his spine, he saw what she so wanted to see.

She was wrong, of course.

'Do you always see the good in people, Bella?' he said, looking at her. *Even when they are not good? Even when they want something from you that you should not have to give?*

She looked confused. 'I just wanted to give you a gift, Raoul. I'm sorry if you don't like it; I just wanted to get you something to remember me by.'

And suddenly every hair on the back of his neck stood up. 'Why would I need something to remember you by? You're not going somewhere?'

'I have to go, Raoul. I've had the best time—really I have—but I'm in your way here; I know. And besides, I have a job to go back to. I can't stay here for ever, after all.'

He had blown it. There was a tightness in his throat, but it was no match for the ball tearing its way through his gut. She had been eating out of the palm of his hand

and he had blown it by leaving her alone because he had had to go to Paris.

No, that wasn't true; he could have handled his business from here, over the phone, could have given his contacts new leads to follow up in their investigations. It was because he had been afraid of getting too close—and now it had cost him. 'When are you planning on leaving?'

'Tomorrow. I've booked my ticket. Marco said he'd take me to the airport.'

So soon!

'Are you mad at me, Bella, for abandoning you today? I knew I should not have left you that way…'

'No, Raoul. It is more than that. This has been a lovely escape, truly, but I need to get back to my life. It is not like we won't see each other again, surely?'

'Of course,' he said, knowing there was no way he could let her return to Paris. Not yet. Garbas would need funds and plenty of them if he was to mount any kind of serious legal defence against the criminal charges already laid against him. He would have his dogs watching. He would know the moment she returned home. And then he would make up some excuse for her about why the charges had been laid in the first place, and ask if she could lend the money from her inheritance to fund his defence.

It wasn't going to happen.

Which meant he could not let her go.

'I'm sorry you feel you must leave,' he said cautiously, careful not to overplay his hand. 'But if that is what you believe you must do…'

'I must go, Raoul,' she said, though her eyes were tinged with sadness, as if she was half-disappointed that he did not argue the point. He took heart from the observation, realising that maybe all was not lost after all. 'My stay in Venice has been wonderful, but I have to return to the real world at some stage.'

'In that case,' he said, knowing that he only had one more shot at this, 'We must not waste a moment of tonight.'

Raoul had suggested formal for the dress code, so she decided on the golden gown Natania had admired that first day that now seemed so long ago. They took a *vaporetto* to Lido, to the five-star Excelsior hotel, a palace of a hotel, no stranger to royalty, film stars and other celebrities. Gabriella tried not to think about how devastating Raoul looked in his black dinner suit but in the end she had to. It was either that or think about how easily Raoul had taken the news she was leaving tomorrow. Maybe he had been expecting it. Maybe even hoping for it.

She wasn't disappointed, she told herself, it was simply validation that she was doing the right thing.

Even if the thought of leaving him hurt like hell.

What had she expected, though? That Raoul would beg her to stay? No, that was pure fantasy. One night in a man's bed didn't mean for ever. Phillipa was right, she needed distance. They both did. She was doing the right thing...

They dined in the restaurant upstairs. Sparkling champagne and the finest wines provided the lubrication, a pianist playing Vivaldi the musical score, and Venice provided the spectacular view—a view that only got better as the sun set behind the city, transforming it into a city of gold. Gabriella forgot about being disappointed because, even though she was going home tomorrow, there could be no better view in the world and no one better to share it with.

After their meal the pianist started playing dance music and Raoul put down his wine glass. 'Dance with me, Bella,' he said, and there was no way she could say no. Why should she? Besides, she was flying home tomorrow; she and Raoul both knew it. There was no reason she should not enjoy tonight.

So she let him take her in his arms and let him masterfully, superbly, spin her around the dance floor until her blood was dizzy. In his arms, she felt his strength and his darkness, and it was hard to separate either, just as it was impossible to separate reality from fantasy. Because this was how she wanted to remember him, a swirling, evocative explosion of feeling.

So they danced, and afterwards she couldn't remember if there had been anyone else on the dance floor with them, absorbed so totally in the man she was dancing with, and it didn't matter because she was with him. He held her close, so close that she could barely breathe, so close that there was no distance between them, no barrier to the growing heat, the building tension as they whirled, entwined, around the dance floor.

Would he take her to bed and make love to her again tonight? She wanted nothing more to end this night, other than a promise to meet again soon. And meanwhile every sensation, every powerful, evocative feeling, was stored away in Gabriella's memory so that until that time she could pull them out and examine them all over again, one by precious one, in the nights when she would inevitably be alone.

Meanwhile, she lost all sense of time. She only knew that the sun had long departed and the moon had risen and she feared the night must come to an end. But he saved her from the end just yet and suggested a walk along the beach before they went home.

She slipped her jewelled sandals off before venturing onto the sand and he offered her his hand so she might carry her sandals and the skirt of her gown without losing balance. She slipped her hand into his. She saw his heated smile and felt his warm grip and let both seep deep into her bones. So what that she was leaving tomorrow? She was going to enjoy every moment of this last night with him.

Just one last night…

The beach was long and almost empty, the season late; what day trippers there had been had long since departed. The beach was theirs, a long strip of sand glowing under the light of the full moon, the air balmy and still, the dark waters laced with silver.

'Did I tell you,' he said after they'd walked hand in hand in companionable silence for some way, 'How beautiful you look tonight?'

Her breath hitched, her heart fluttered in her chest like a winged beast. 'No,' she said. 'I don't believe you did.'

'Then I am remiss. So let me tell you now.' He stopped

walking then and turned to her. 'Tonight you are more beautiful than I have ever seen you. More beautiful than the sun setting over the most beautiful city in the world, more beautiful than the pearl of a moon hanging heavy in the sky.'

There was so much power in his words, so much depth and feeling, that her heart almost burst from her chest to embrace him. But at the same time she knew she dared not believe him. 'Thank you, Raoul, but I wish you wouldn't say such things.'

'Why shouldn't I tell you what I think?'

'Because I am leaving tomorrow, and you will only make it harder—for me, at least.'

'Then don't leave.'

She laughed a little uncertainly and turned, starting to walk back the other way. 'We've been through this. I have to go. I can't stay here for ever.'

'And what about what happened last night? Didn't that mean anything to you?'

'Hey, I wasn't the one who left this morning without saying goodbye.'

'I knew you were angry with me.'

'No. I'm not angry.' She thought about the talk she'd had with Phillipa earlier today, the sense her friend had made, even though the thought of leaving and missing out on more nights like she'd spent last night... But, no, space and distance were what she needed now. Head space. Physical distance. 'Last night was amazing. But everything has happened so quickly, I need some time to work it all out. To work out what I want.'

He took her hand and squeezed it. 'I understand.'

They walked a little way to the sound of the sea lapping at the shore, music and laughter wafting on the breeze from a party somewhere up the coast, and she thought that was the end of the matter until he said, 'Can I let you in on a secret?'

She turned to him. 'Of course.'

He stopped her and took her hand to his mouth, pressing his lips against her palm, sending a sizzle all the way to her toes. 'A long time ago, I made a promise to myself. Last night, in your bed, I was tempted to break it.'

She shook her head, confused, laughing just a little to try to ease the tension. 'I'm not sure I understand.'

'You see, I do not break promises easily. And wanting to break a promise made me hurt you, I think, by leaving this morning without a word.'

'You had business, you said.'

'I did. But I did not have to leave you to do it. I was afraid of what might happen if I stayed.'

'Raoul,' she said, her heart tripping, 'What are you saying?'

'A long time ago I vowed never to marry again. I promised myself that I would never take another wife. But last night, in your bed, I came close to breaking that vow—so close that it scared me.'

Every cell in her body froze; her lungs squeezed tight, so tight she could barely get out the words. 'I don't think I understand.'

'I panicked this morning. I behaved stupidly and left you, and I hurt you and made you angry when that was the last thing I wanted to do. What I really wanted to do was ask you, Bella, if you would do me the honour of becoming my wife.'

'Raoul...'

'I know I don't deserve it, Bella. I know I am the last person you would want to marry, and the least deserving, but would you consider my proposal anyway? Would you marry me?'

'You're serious. You're actually serious.'

'I have never been more serious in my life.'

She looked up at him, his eyes so intent that for a second she was tempted—oh, so tempted—to fall into those dark depths and believe him.

But, no! She shook her head and started walking down the beach away from him, her heart thumping like a drum, making so much noise it was no surprise she couldn't think straight. 'Raoul, that's just crazy.'

'Don't you think I know that?' she heard him call. 'Don't you see why I couldn't face you this morning?'

No. She couldn't think. And she couldn't see that. She couldn't see anything, not with the sudden tears streaming down her face as she stumbled along the sand.

She wasn't even sure what she was running from. Didn't she want Raoul to want her? Except that it almost seemed too much, too soon. Too perfect. Too imperfect. Oh God, what should she believe?

'Bella!' he yelled, catching her arm, pulling her to him.

'You didn't want me here,' she remembered as she slammed into his hard chest. 'You never wanted me to come to Venice in the first place, and yet now you tell me you want to marry me?' She punched him on the arm, on the shoulder, would have punched him on his chin if his wrist hadn't snagged hers and dragged it down where her fist could do no damage. 'So what are you trying to prove by asking me to marry you?'

'What are *you* trying to prove? I've told you I want to marry you. Why do you fight that? After the night we shared, why can't you believe that?'

She shook her head. 'That was one night! We need more time. It's too soon.'

'I thought it was too soon. How could I think of breaking a promise I had made for life after such a short time with you? Don't you think I have tortured myself all day for leaving you like I did? For leaving you thinking I didn't care?

'But let me make it plain—this is not about one night. Because I wanted you the moment I first set eyes on you. I wanted you then, Bella. I want you now. And I am willing to break every vow I have ever made in my life to have you, if you will only have me.'

'But wouldn't it be more sensible to wait?'

'Why wait, when we feel this way? Why live apart when we are made to be together? Because if I am not mistaken you feel it too, don't you? You feel this magic between us. Do you really believe this is going to go away? Why should we wait when we are so good together?'

There was something exciting about his words, something urgent and powerful that tugged on that part of her that wanted to believe him. Wanted to believe his words were true—maybe because they so closely mirrored her own feelings.

She didn't really want to leave. Logic told her she should, but her heart would always stay here with Raoul, no matter how far she moved, no matter where she lived.

But *still* he hadn't said the words that she so wanted to hear. 'You tell me how much I mean to you, and yet you haven't told me that you love me.'

'Haven't I?' He took her in his arms and kissed her then, so deep and deliciously that it felt like his kiss had touched her very soul and sworn his love. 'But then, if I didn't love you, why else would I want to marry you?'

He kissed her again and she knew she had not imagined it the first time—that there was no way he could not love her, not when his kiss touched her so deeply, not when she knew in her heart he was the man for her.

It might be crazy, rash and all kinds of madness, but it was a madness they clearly both shared—and what point was logic and waiting when what you wanted was clearly right?

'You are really sure about this?' she asked one final time to be sure of what he was asking. 'You really are serious about wanting to marry me?'

'I have never been more serious in my life.'

And the zipper of heat that flushed out from her spine confirmed that she had no choice, no choice at all…

'Then I will marry you, Raoul. Please, yes, I will marry you.'

'I so wish Umberto could be here,' she mused as Phillipa handed her the bouquet, a glorious rose concoction in soft apricot, peach and cream colours from which long ribbons fluttered. It was two minutes before the wedding ceremony was due to get underway and they were expecting a knock at the door at any moment to let them know it was time. Meanwhile she had time to think about Umberto and a moment they had both missed out on.

'He would be so proud of you,' Phillipa said.

Gabriella could only agree. Umberto would have had no objections to her marrying Raoul. He would have approved wholeheartedly, no doubt, which was some consolation, given he was not here to give her away. She just wished he could be here to see how she looked today.

The beaded gown clung to her body like a second skin and the hours she'd put in today at the spa and hair salon had been well worth it. Her skin was smooth, her nails perfectly manicured and her hair had been pulled up into a classic style, sleek and polished, with a few tendrils coiling around her face, a face that today even she conceded came close to beautiful. That was probably more due to the fact she couldn't stop smiling rather than her perfectly applied make-up, but whatever it was it was working.

Today she felt like a princess from some long-ago fairy tale about to marry her fairy-tale prince. And the only thing that could have made her feel better was her grandfather being here to see her get married.

'Strange, really, how it was Umberto's death that brought Raoul and me together. Do you think he'll be here somewhere today watching over us?'

'I know he will. And he will be as happy for you as the rest of us are.'

She smiled as she looked down at the bouquet. 'You

know, I really thought you might try to talk me out of marrying Raoul, but you've been fantastic. Thank you.'

'Why on earth do you say such things?'

'Because you told me to wait and to take my time, and now I've gone and done neither. I thought you'd be lining up to tell me I'm about to make the mistake of my life.'

Her friend laughed. 'Okay, so I thought you were being rash and I was worried about you. But I've seen you with Raoul, and do you really think I would interfere in anything, or in your dealings with anyone, who had obviously made you so happy? It is clear Raoul loves you with all his heart.'

Gabriella wrapped her arm around her friend and squeezed her tight, for she had needed to hear that. 'Thank you so much for that. Because it is crazy, how fast this has all happened. But I love him so much. I love him with all my heart. I want to spend the rest of my life with him.'

She turned away then, pretending to be interested in the sparkle of the diamond-encrusted pearl earrings in her lobes, wondering where the hell the knock on the door she was waiting for to tell her it was time to start the ceremony was, knowing she should take courage from her friend's words.

It is clear Raoul loves you with all his heart.

Was it clear? She wanted it to be true. Because still he had not said the words to her. And then she thought again of the words he had said to her, letting them lend her strength…

Some things do not need to be said for us to know them to be true.

And she knew he would say it. He was just waiting for the right moment. *Like tonight.*

A sizzle of raw heat slid down her spine and sparked a fire deep in her belly. Tonight they would consummate their marriage in that place where it had first happened, under the lover's alcove.

She could hardly wait.

She heard a knock on her door and felt a hand on her arm, seeing Phillipa in the reflection in the mirror. 'It's time,' her friend said.

The chapel was lit with burnished golden light, the sun already descending over Venice and gilding the assembled guests. There weren't a lot, not that Gabriella noticed anything once she saw Raoul standing at the front waiting for her, his hair blue-black under the light, slicked back into his signature ponytail, his dark suit showing his height and the breadth of his shoulders to perfection.

And, although she believed in Raoul with all her heart, although she knew that he loved her, still she looked for some kind of sign—something to confirm that she was not acting crazy, agreeing to marry a man so quickly. Something to confirm he was the man she wanted, who wanted her.

She watched him say something to Marco standing alongside him, when the music heralding her entrance started. Marco glanced up and stopped him with just a tap to his shoulder and a nod, and Raoul stilled and turned around.

Their eyes meet across the small chapel and she felt the impact of his like a blast of heat. *Raoul*, her soul seemed to whisper, relief infusing every part of her as their gazes tangled and meshed, knowing nobody could look at her that way unless he truly loved her. Unless he was her soul mate. Nobody else could make her feel so alive, so desired.

Phillipa turned to her and beamed. 'Oh my God,' she said. 'Did you see the way he looked at you? This guy is seriously in love.' And then she threw her smile and turned, setting off slowly down the aisle.

'I now pronounce you man and wife. You may kiss the bride.'

It was done.

Raoul felt the rush of success lift the weight of a promise made to a dying man clean from his shoulders in a tidal surge. But then he made the mistake of looking down at his new bride, who was watching him through that veil with those damned cat-like eyes, anticipating his kiss, full of expectant hopes, dreams and wishes; the tide crashed right back over him.

'I love you,' she mouthed and he wanted to run right then and there from the chapel. Guilt crashed over him. Hadn't he done enough? He'd married her, hadn't he?

He'd never wanted her love.

But people were waiting; the priest was waiting, and she was waiting. She looked more like a goddess than any woman had a right to, every diamond hanging from her ear, every bead on her dress, even the moisture in her eyes, catching the light so that she sparkled before him like a glass of fine champagne waiting to be sipped.

So he forced himself to smile. Forced himself to look at her like a man who had realised his ultimate dream and had not just fulfilled a promise to a dying friend. He lifted the veil that separated them and dipped his head, curling a hand around her slim neck and trying not to think about how good she felt under his hand, how taut her skin was, how smooth. Then they kissed and he tried not to think about how good she tasted—sweet, ripe and willing. While the 'willing' was difficult enough to forget, it was her whispered, "I love you," that tortured him the most.

Because she wouldn't love him when this was over.

She would never speak to him again.

She would hate him for ever.

Anticipation bubbled in her veins as Raoul handed her into the *vaporetto* and then tucked her in beside him. The wedding and reception had been everything she'd ever dreamed of and more, every little girl's fantasy come true. And now she was anticipating a wedding night that was her big-girl fantasy come true, the night she'd been dreaming of ever since he had proposed those few long weeks ago.

It was late, the moon already wearying of the night, and she didn't mind at first that he had little to say. They'd spent a night talking, laughing and being congratulated, barely having time to speak to each other. So it was good to have the time to sit in the curve of his arm and contemplate the coming pleasures.

With every passing minute she felt anticipation coil and grow inside her. Tonight they would once again join the parade of nymphs, satyrs, gods and goddesses engaged in the act of love. The thought brought a secret smile to her face. She snuggled in closer to her new husband, breathing in his signature scent, relishing it, knowing that from tonight it was just one more pleasure at her disposal.

'I love your scent,' she murmured, nestling closer, thinking about returning to the *palazzo* and spending their wedding night in each other's arms in the lover's alcove. 'I don't think I'll ever get enough of it.'

Something about the way his body stiffened and shifted against her made her look up. She noticed the lights around them looked wrong; they seemed to be heading away from Venice instead of towards it.

'Where are we going?' she asked, curiosity getting the better of her.

'The airport.'

'Raoul,' she said, half-disappointed they were not going straight home to the apartment, half-delighted that he had gone to some trouble to make this night special. 'You actually planned a honeymoon and you didn't tell me? Where are we going?'

'Spain.'

'Tonight?' she said with a tinge of regret. 'But it's already so late, and I was hoping…'

'It's not far,' he said abruptly, apparently more interested in looking out to sea in the direction they were going than looking at her, and letting whatever she was hoping slide right on by. 'You can sleep on the plane.'

She swallowed down the bubble of disappointment. It was thoughtful that he'd wanted to surprise her, really it was, but she didn't want to sleep on a plane. Not tonight. Not when she'd been hoping that soon she would be once again lying with her new husband in her big, wide bed—*their* big, wide bed—amongst the nymphs and satyrs, joining them once again in their endless celebrations of the flesh, only this time as a married couple.

But, while it was sweet he'd wanted to find somewhere more special for their first married night together, something seemed wrong.

'Is everything okay?'

'Of course'

'Are you sure? Something seems to be bothering you.'

'It's nothing,' he said.

And then she remembered. 'Didn't your family have a place somewhere in Spain once?' she asked, remembering a snippet from her past. His head snapped around towards her, but before she could read anything in his eyes his mobile phone rang.

He pulled it from his pocket and checked the caller ID before holding the phone up to his ear and turning away. 'Excuse me, I must take this call…'

Gabriella jerked awake as the car came to a halt. She'd slept fitfully, first on the charter jet and then in the back of the car that had been waiting for them at the airport when they had landed.

'We're here,' Raoul said beside her. She stretched and blinked, wondering where the resort was when she could see nothing through the gloom and swirling mist except a glimpse of grey stone walls that were just as quickly swallowed up again.

She yawned, bone weary, wondering what time it was as a light snapped on somewhere, turning the outside world a glaring white as her door was pulled open. 'Marco,' she said, shivering as he helped her alight to the misty outside world, a world that carried the scent of salt and sea and the sound of surf crashing somewhere nearby. 'How did you get here so quickly?'

He nodded. 'Natania and I left straight after the ceremony to get things ready. Welcome, Signora del Arco.' Through her weariness shot a burst of pleasure. She was a married woman now and the idea was still so novel it sent a thrill coursing through her. A married woman, as of tonight—soon to be married in every sense of the word. She shivered again, this time less due to the cold and more to the anticipation of what was still to come.

'Did you hear that, Raoul?' she said, looking around for him, but he mustn't have heard or was thinking about something else—because he was scowling, his features tight as he rounded the car from the other side.

'Get the luggage, Marco,' he snapped, before turning perfunctorily to her. 'It's cold out here. Let's go inside.'

Something was definitely on his mind, she gathered. He'd been abrupt ever since they'd left the wedding. Or maybe he was just as tired as she. Still, she wished for the warmth of his arm around her or even the warm gesture of walking hand in hand. She realised he had barely touched her since the *vaporetto* trip across the water. 'What is this place?' she asked, still wearing her heels and cautiously following him up a short flight of ancient stone steps worn low by the footprints of a hundred generations. 'Where exactly are we?'

'Galicia,' he said. 'On the Atlantic coast of Spain.'

Around them the mist swirled, danced and kissed her bare skin with cold, damp lips, while above them rose high stone walls that looked grim and austere and that disappeared into the fog. The surf continued to crash unseen somewhere below.

A door opened before them, massive and heavy with enormous iron fittings. Natania was there to welcome them into the massive entrance hall, looking rumpled and sexy, but sullen with it, as though their arrival had inconveniently interrupted the other couple and she'd had to hastily pull her clothes back on.

'Do you want something to eat?' she asked unconvincingly, looking from one to the other. Gabriella waited, hoping Raoul would say they were going straight to bed.

'You show Gabriella to her room,' he surprised her by saying instead. 'I'll be in the study. Unless,' he said, turning to her, 'You're hungry?'

She was too shocked for a moment to respond and she wasn't sure what bothered her more: the talk of *her* room instead of *ours*, or the fact he was not coming with her. 'Not at all, but...'

'Then Natania will show you upstairs. You must be tired.' He kissed her on the cheek, a platonic kiss, a benevolent kiss. A kiss that went nowhere near to being the kind of kiss she was looking for this night of all nights. 'I will see you in the morning. Sleep well.'

'This way,' Natania said, bangles jangling on her

wrists as she headed for a curving staircase, a sound that jangled on Gabriella's already shot nerves. But there was no way she was going to follow the woman when her new husband was already going in the other direction.

'Raoul!' she said, her heels clicking on the flagstone floor. She caught up with him halfway across the floor, took his arm and attempted a smile and a laugh, as if there had been some kind of mistake. There *had* to have been some kind of mistake. 'It's our wedding night, Raoul. Surely you're not going to spend it in the study working all night?'

Something in his expression softened. He touched a hand to her hair. 'I'm sorry, Bella.' It was the first time, she realised, he had used his pet name for her today. 'But it is very late and there is something I must attend to. And I thought you would appreciate a rest after our long day.'

'Can't it wait?'

'No.'

'Then I will wait for you, Raoul. You have to sleep some time.'

He just looked at her, and his dark eyes looked so empty it chilled her all the way to her bones. 'As you wish.'

She pushed up on her toes and kissed him on the lips, brazenly letting her breasts press against his chest, lingering there so could be in no way unclear as to whether she would rather sleep or make love, no matter how long his work took or what time he came in. 'I wish.'

Natania was waiting for her on the stairs, her dark gypsy eyes missing nothing of the exchange.

'He'll come up when he's finished,' Gabriella said with a brightness she had to plaster on to make stick. 'If you just show me the way.'

Natania said nothing, merely performed a slow blink of her wide eyes and turned to lead the way up the long staircase, her bangles again sounding too bright and discordant for the grim setting and Gabriella's equally grim mood.

A long gallery met them lined with heavy drapes, heavier furniture and paintings of windswept cliffs and boiling seas. A castle featured in one, severe and solid, complete with battlements and turrets, clinging to the edge of the cliff like it was part of it. This castle? she wondered. It could be, judging from the interior, dark and brooding, like a slumbering giant waiting for the light. Not exactly the honeymoon resort she'd been anticipating. Then again, she thought with a pang of hurt, so far this was nothing like a honeymoon.

'What is this place?' she asked, catching Natania up outside a door.

'Castillo Del Arco,' she said, leading her into the big high-ceilinged room. 'It is, Raoul's *other* place.'

'It's very—grand,' she said, wondering how she could subtly ask where her husband's room was.

'I hate it,' the other woman said. 'It is a bad place.'

Gabriella wandered into the vast room. So this was to be *her* room. Clearly it was not Raoul's. It was too soft, with its patterned wallpaper and rich, red velvet curtains; a fireplace lit with gold flames ran along one wall, a four-poster bed standing proudly against its opposite, an ornately carved blanket box at its foot. There was a door alongside the bed, and she opened it, curious to see if it led into Raoul's room —hoping—and immediately was disappointed when she found only an en suite.

Natania's words finally wormed their way into her consciousness. She spun around, reminded of Phillipa's warning in the frisson of fear that ran down her spine. 'Bad? In what way?'

But Natania wasn't listening. Marco had arrived with the luggage someone else had clearly packed for her and he was leaning down, kissing her.

Gabriella disappeared into the bathroom, feeling simultaneously shocked, breathless and guilty that she had witnessed the intimacy, even though logic told her she had done nothing wrong. *I'm just tired*, she told herself; *strung out*. She took a couple of deep breaths while she ran cold water over her wrists, willing the colour in her face to subside.

But there was no way she could will away her own desires, or the buzz of need that bloomed, insistent and pulsing, deep in her belly and tight in her breasts. For it should be Raoul with *his* mouth on *hers*; Raoul in her bedroom.

Damn.

Marco had left when she returned; Natania was busy unpacking her luggage. 'There's no point doing that,' she told her. 'We'll only have to repack it all when I shift rooms tomorrow.' *Because there was no way she intended to let herself be shunted off into her own room another night.* 'Right now I just want to crawl into bed.' Natania's eyes flared with a wild flame that told her that was exactly what Natania intended herself—except she would not be spending the night alone in hers.

'If you are sure…'

Gabriella just nodded, the beginning of a headache tugging at her temples. 'You go.' *At least one of us might as well have a good night.* She was just leaving when Gabriella remembered. 'Natania, what did you mean when you said this was a bad place?'

The other woman gave her a look of such abject pity that she was almost crushed under the weight of it. 'I am sorry, I should not have spoken of such things. Good night.' And with that she was gone.

What things?

She prowled the room, wanting to shriek at the closed door, at the walls, the bed and the rich, dark drapes. She wanted to shriek with the insanity of it all. This was her wedding night. *Her wedding night!* And yet here she was, tucked away in a lonely room in a castle on some godforsaken stretch of coastline shrouded in mist.

And where the hell was her husband?

She threw off her sandals and flung them across the room, where they smacked into the wall and it was still nowhere near satisfying enough.

What the hell did he think he was doing?

Nobody worked on their wedding night. Nobody!

Thunder boomed in the distance, a low, rumbling growl that went on and on and echoed her own rumbling discontent. A flash of lightning painted the room with the curtains' vivid red.

Damn it! Natania would know where he was. She should just have asked her. Barefoot, she rushed to the door and pulled it open to the darkened hallway. She could see nothing and nobody, until another clap of thunder that seemed to shake the very walls was followed by a light so bright it transformed night into day.

And there, at the end of the long passageway, she saw a shadowy figure—*Natania?*—disappearing into a room.

She called out to her but the sound was lost in the sudden crash of rain on the windows and the doors as the castle descended once again into blackness, only a thin, ghostly glow through a window at the end of the passageway providing any illumination.

She wanted to follow the woman, but right now she was probably already in the arms, if not the bed, of Marco. Did she really need to interrupt them in the act of love-making? Did she really need to remind herself of what she herself would have been doing—*should have been doing*—if only her husband had not decided to abandon her on their wedding night?

What would they think of her? The lonely bride, still in her wedding gown, searching desperately for her husband.

She had seen the pity in Natania's eyes. Did she really need to see more?

The rain pelted down on the roof and walls until the pounding itself sounded like thunder. She shivered. It was freezing out here in the dark passageway; her head was thumping and she was tired beyond measure. Bone weary. Across the room the fire crackled in the hearth;

the bed looked cosy and inviting. And down the end of the passage the thin, grey light was just a shade lighter. It was later than she thought. It would be dawn soon.

No wonder she was so tired. She would lie down for a while to get warm. And maybe Raoul would come to her when he had finished his work like she had asked him to. She would wait up for him.

And tomorrow—*today*—things would make more sense. They had to.

He stood at the rain-streaked windows, looking out into the bleak nothingness of the storm, wishing bleak nothingness for his mind to erase all thoughts of the woman lying upstairs waiting for him.

Right now she would be confused and angry. He could deal with those things, he expected them. It was the hurt he could not deal with; the hurt he knew she must be feeling.

But she was tired, she would sleep. And soon she would understand that this was the way it had to be.

'It is done, Umberto,' he said, gazing unseeingly into the night through the rain-streaked windows. 'And I hope you are satisfied.'

CHAPTER EIGHT

HE HADN'T come.

It was after midday when she awakened to the sound of Natania bringing in a tray, and the sickening, hollow feeling that Raoul had not come to her bed.

Natania swished open the long curtains with a flourish to reveal a bright blue sky and turned to watch her through hooded eyes. 'Raoul asked me to check on you.'

'That was very considerate of him,' Gabriella said snippily, her disappointment turning to anger, thinking it might have been just a tad nicer if Raoul had come to check on her himself. 'And how is my husband today?'

The woman gave a lazy shrug. 'I have learned not to ask such questions.'

'Because you don't like the answers?'

'Because sometimes it is better not to know.'

Gabriella didn't agree. She had a few questions she intended to ask, and she wanted to know the answers. She padded to the window while Natania poured the coffee, and her gaze was met by a scene of staggering beauty. The castle was built on some kind of rocky headland with a small sandy cove off to one side. Below them the sea foamed white onto the rocks at the foot of the cliff, a sea lit with sparkling diamonds and so dazzlingly blue, it rivalled the brilliant sky for supremacy. Everything looked bright and calm and perfect.

So different from last night with the fog and the storm; maybe she had been overly tired and feeling melodramatic with it. Already she felt better, brighter, just for feeling the warmth of the day through the glass. She would feel much better again when she had talked to Raoul.

Armed with Natania's directions to the library, and feeling refreshed after breakfast and a bath, she wandered the passageways of the labyrinthine castle. Even in daylight it was a gloomy place, filled with dark timber furniture, beams and heavy wall-hangings, all seemingly impenetrable to the outside sunshine. She shivered in her sundress and light cardigan—a choice inspired by the sunny view from her window rather than the ambient temperature—and wondered if it ever warmed up inside.

There was hush all around her, no other signs of life, and only the tick of a grandfather clock at the top of the stairs intruded on the silence, jarring her nerves as she wended her way slowly down the long staircase. She treaded lightly, careful not to make any noise herself, feeling like she must comply, and only hesitated when she neared the bottom step, knowing the sound of her low heels on the flagstones would echo in this vast space. So unnaturally quiet it was almost as if the castle, that sleeping giant from last night, was awake and waiting, holding its breath, and she didn't want to be the one to make it spring into action…

Suddenly there was the creak of a door, a bang. And so lost was she in her quiet world that she jumped and gasped.

'Gabriella! There you are, at last,' Raoul said, smiling as he strode towards her. 'I thought you were going to sleep all day.'

He took both her hands and kissed her cheeks, and she drank in his scent, letting it feed into her soul, letting it comfort her. And here, two steps up, so she could look him in the eyes, she told him, 'I waited for you.'

He tilted his head, a lock of his black hair falling free from his ponytail and curling around his eyes, his expression truly contrite. 'I'm sorry, Bella.' He used his pet name for her again at last, giving her a glimpse of the man she thought she had married. 'I finished way too late. I didn't want to disturb you.'

And in the rational light of day her concerns of last night seemed overblown, exaggerated.

'Come on,' he said, taking her hand. 'How about I give you a tour so you can find your way around? And then I suggest lunch down in the cove where the wind will not bother us. Natania has promised to make us a picnic basket.'

It all sounded so wonderful—Raoul sounded so wonderful—that Gabriella just laughed, feeling the weight of last night's worries float away.

The castle was even larger than she had anticipated, stretching from one length of the headland to the other. One side of the central staircase was given over to a massive feasting room, big-beamed and with a central fireplace on which it would be possible to roast an entire ox. The library where Raoul had his office set up was an incongruous blend of technology atop antique desks and cabinets, its walls stacked so high with books that he had to practically drag Gabriella out of it, in order to show her the rest of the house, with promises she could visit and explore whenever she wanted.

Upstairs he showed her room after room; there must be a dozen bedrooms and just as many bathrooms, so many with their furniture covered in dust covers. She had to concede she had been given the prettiest of them all, which was still no consolation. *Which one is yours?* she itched to ask; *where do you sleep?* But she wanted him to surprise her and show her and invite her inside and make her his wife…

'And this one is Natania's room?' she said, wanting to speed up the tour in her quest to find his when they reached the end of the hallway.

'No. Natania sleeps downstairs. There's an annexe above the garage she and Marco share.'

'But I saw her last night during the storm. I called out to her but she didn't hear me.'

Every hair on the back of his neck stood up. She reached for the handle before he could stop her. 'It's locked,' she said, turning to him. 'Do you have the key?'

'It's nothing but a store room,' he said coarsely, tugging her away. 'Nobody uses it. Come, let's go. Lunch will be ready.'

He excused himself at the bottom of the stairs, showed her how to find the kitchen and told her he'd meet her there in a few moments, before striding towards the library.

She found the kitchen where he'd indicated, Natania packing their lunch into the basket, Marco by her side helping. They were a team, the two of them, almost inseparable; she stopped dead, feeling like an intruder again. *Feeling jealous.* Not of Natania, exactly, for she wasn't interested in Marco. But she wanted to feel Raoul close by her side, wanted to enjoy such simple intimacies with him.

'So you found him?' Natania said, noticing her, brushing her hands together and setting her gypsy bangles jangling before she reached for a bowl of salad topped with fat red tomatoes.

'Thank you, yes; he's just gone to get something.'

'You will like the cove,' she said. 'It is very private. Very intimate. You can swim naked and nobody will see you.'

If Gabriella blushed any more she was likely to end up in the salad instead of eating it. 'Good to know. Maybe when it's warmer.'

'You would be surprised. It is very protected from the wind. And some men cannot resist a taste of bare flesh.' She shrugged her bare shoulder, smiling at Marco, whose eyes were glinting with heated agreement. For all their shared secrets, Gabriella got the distinct impression the other woman was giving her advice.

Would she take it? Maybe she wouldn't need to. Maybe Raoul had been planning sinful seduction for this afternoon the whole time; maybe that was why he'd decided on the picnic. 'I'll keep that in mind,' she said as Raoul joined them.

'What will you keep in mind?'

'That the mist and storms blow in quickly,' Natania said, looking levelly at Gabriella. 'To watch out for them.' Gabriella felt almost like she had found an unexpected ally.

'The weather is perfect. There will be no storms today.' He picked up the basket. 'Let's go.'

Natania pressed a blanket into her hands. 'Take this. It is not good to get sand in your food.'

The sultry images that advice put into her head had her halfway to blushing again, but then she suddenly remembered. 'Oh, Natania, Raoul says that door at the end of the corridor is locked, but you must have a key—I thought I saw you go in there last night.'

The atmosphere in the room chilled to ice as the two exchanged glances, Marco standing stiffly alongside; she wondered what it was she'd said wrong.

'I was not there last night.'

'But I saw you, after you came to my room. Well, I *thought* I saw you, when the lightning struck. I called your name, but you mustn't have heard me over the sound of the storm.'

'No. I went straight downstairs after leaving your room. You could not have seen me.'

'Oh.'

'Forget it,' said Raoul, his voice thick and gruff. 'It was obviously just the drapes moving in the wind and making shadows, that's all. Let's go.'

It was not possible, he told himself as he led her along the path towards the stone steps leading down to the beach. It was impossible, he knew, but still he had needed to

check. There had been nothing in the room to say anyone had been there, let alone her. There was no way it
could be possible. Katia was his ghost, his nightmare.

Although not his only nightmare now.

For now he had another one, and this one was of his
own creation.

He'd headed off her questions when he'd met her at
the bottom of the stairs. He'd been expecting a fight, or
at least some kind of remonstration about her having
been expected to sleep alone. It had to come at some
time. It would come. Nothing was surer.

And all he was doing now by taking her to lunch and
treating her as she deserved to be treated was delaying
the inevitable, hoping to draw out this time with her as
long as possible. She had to believe this marriage was
real, at least until Garbas was put away for good.

But there was a far more selfish reason for wanting
to be with her—because it was impossible to abandon
her completely, even though he knew that, the way he
burned for her, it would be a safer course of action to
do so. Maybe this way would draw the pain out longer,
cause them both unnecessary torture, but there had to be
some benefit for doing what he was doing for Umberto,
some pay off other than knowing she was safe from the
likes of Garbas.

He wanted her near. He knew he was playing with
fire, but he wanted that pay off. He wanted more of those
moments with her to remember and to hold with him for
ever long after she'd discovered what he was really like
or why he had really married her and was long gone. For
she would leave him, that was for sure.

And that knowledge alone was enough to clamp his gut.

'I thought your family used to live in Barcelona.' They were halfway down the path to the beach before she spoke—maybe because he'd taken off like the devil himself. 'I'm sure we visited you all there one year.'

He turned, wondering how much she remembered. 'We did.'

'You don't live there now?'

'No.'

'You sold it?'

He wished. As it was, he could barely remember that night long ago when he had been so furious with the world and the hand it had dealt him, so unprepared for dealing with his own inadequacies. 'I lost it in a card game.'

'Oh.'

'You win some, you lose some.' The phrase came nowhere near to describing the pain he'd felt on losing the property at the time. He'd thought himself indestructible. Invincible. That had made him the worst kind of fool. Even now his failure, his sheer recklessness, appalled him. The knowledge of those wasted years was like a millstone around his neck, weighing him down. He had learned to rationalise his loss since then, see it for what it was, a moment in time when he'd made both some bad decisions and some good. But it didn't make him feel any better about it.

'Like your apartment in Venice?'

He shrugged, wishing himself a past that was one whole lot more glorious. 'Exactly like Venice.'

'And this place? Another card game? Another win?'

He looked back over his shoulder, up at the castle that imposed itself on the clifftop almost as if it were part of it. He realised the truth, maybe for the first time in his life, and only because of what he was doing to her—he hated this place.

Was that why he had brought her here? Not from some noble desire to keep her safe, but so he might taint thoughts of her with this toxic castle and its toxic memories? So it might make it easier when she left?

Or because it was easier for him to remember why he was wrong for her? Because a man who did not hold out a hand to a woman in desperate need...

She deserved better.

She was like a breath of fresh air in a stale room. She was a candle glowing in a dark cave.

And it crushed him like a weight on his chest that, for all he had given her, he might be the one to extinguish that light.

'Another win,' he conceded, although it hardly seemed a win now when it was the last place he wanted to be with Gabriella. She should be somewhere far more deserving of her company right now. Somewhere light, beautiful and free from the darkness of the past. And she should be with someone far more worthy.

But she was with him now, and there was a picnic waiting, the curve of sand in the cove lying inviting below. If he could not give her happiness, he could at least give her a taste of what she deserved.

He turned, holding out his hand to her as they negotiated the first of the uneven stone steps down to the beach, and she smiled her thanks, her hand warm and surprisingly strong in his. Surprisingly addictive. He wished it could be more than just her hand he held, and for a moment he just looked at her.

The soft breeze tugged at her fringe over those smiling, brandy-coloured eyes, toyed with the skirt of her white sundress, kicking up the hem around her long, tan legs. For a moment he almost forgot himself and thought about taking her into his arms and crushing her to him, wanting to possess her in every sense of the word.

'Raoul,' she whispered. He saw her mouth form the word and for the first time he noticed how good his name looked on her lips.

And he turned away, setting off down the stairs, knowing he could not afford to notice such details, knowing there was no point to it. But he would accept her smiles and laughter. He would take them and store them away in a special place in his mind so that, once she was gone, he could take them out, dust them off and remember how precious it had been to have her if only for such a short time…

The beach was as protected as Natania had promised, the cove acting like a sun trap, the air still and surprisingly warm. Gabriella kicked off her sandals and wiggled her toes in the sand. Delicious.

Just like Raoul's gaze had been moments before. She was still half-breathless with its impact, still dizzy with the anticipation and the desire.

He wanted her. And that knowledge made her body bloom in readiness. Was that why he had brought her here, to seduce her on the sandy shore today, before they joined as a married couple tonight?

The cove was larger than you could tell from the castle, full of secret grottoes hidden behind giant boulders so they were utterly private. She glanced up at the castle where it sat heavy and imposing on the cliff, recognising it from the painting in the hall near her room. She mentally counted rooms, working out which one was her bedroom, checking out the angles from where the kitchen must be, frowning when she noticed the turret.

'What's that room?' she asked. 'The one with the turret?'

He shook his head without bothering to look that way. 'Nothing. A store room.'

'It must be somewhere over that locked door. Are there stairs inside?'

'Perhaps. It is not something I bother to think about. Do you want to eat?'

She squeezed her eyes against the light and put a hand up to shade her brow, trying to make out details. 'The view from there must be wonderful.'

'How about the view from here?' he suggested, and she turned back to him to see. He had found a place bathed in the warmth of the sun and yet totally private from any inquisitive eyes at the castle. Not that she imagined Natania and Marco would be bothered to watch them when the pair were clearly more involved in each other. They laid the blanket down upon the virgin sand and set the picnic basket in the middle.

'I hope you're hungry,' he said. 'Natania has prepared an entire feast.'

He pulled out a plate of chicken, a dish of plump, green olives stuffed with feta, another plate of cheese, some crusty bread and the rustic salad. Everything looked and smelt delicious; she was more than hungry, but food was not her greatest need at this time.

She accepted a glass of the local village wine, though, ruby-red and spun with gold in the afternoon sun. And she lay sideways on the blanket, one arm propping up her head, the other hand nursing the wine glass. She didn't have large breasts but she knew the angle would spill them together and accentuate their curves. She was determined to seduce him, if he didn't seduce her first.

'How long have Marco and Natania worked for you?'

'Ten years,' he said, selecting one of the fat olives. 'Maybe longer. Maybe shorter. Why do you ask?'

'They seem very close.'

'They have been together much longer than they have been with me.'

'They clearly love each other very much.'

He did not look at her, she noticed. He did not take the opportunity to say he loved her, as she hoped he might. Instead he looked out to sea. 'Perhaps. It is not my business.'

'You mean you haven't seen them together? They're very affectionate. Very—*close*.'

'They do their work. That is all I ask.'

'He is very good-looking, of course.'

He looked at her now, she noted with satisfaction as she sipped on her wine. He had taken no time at all to swing his head around to her. 'Who is?'

'Marco, of course. I can see what Natania sees in him.'

He picked up a small pebble from the sand and flung it at the sea where it landed with a plop. 'You find Marco attractive?'

She shrugged. 'Maybe I like what he does for Natania. I like the way he is so fascinated in her, so drawn to her. She seems happy enough.'

He didn't answer, just turned his gaze out to sea again. She propped her glass in the sand, slipped off her cardigan and flicked her hair off her neck. 'That's better. It's warm here. Natania said it was warm enough in the cove to swim naked.'

'I wouldn't know.'

'Maybe we should give it a try.'

'The water will be freezing.'

'I can think of a way we can warm up afterwards.' She sat up and popped the first two buttons on her dress. 'I'm game if you are.'

His arm snaked out, his wrist ensnaring hers like a manacle before she could attempt the third. His eyes were dark and storm-tossed. 'Don't do this, Gabriella.'

'Don't do what?'

'What you're doing.'

But she refused to give in that easily. She knew he wanted her; he just had to see it. 'I thought you liked to see me naked?' she said innocently enough, her words couched as an invitation, designed to inflame him.

'Anyone might see you.'

She shook her head, unwound his fingers from her wrist and took them to her mouth, kissing each one in turn, sucking them, rolling her tongue around each fingertip, a blatant promise. 'Not here,' she said, taking his

hand lower, curling his fingers around the third button, popping another so her bodice parted and exposed a wide wedge of her breasts that she held the palm of his hand against. 'We're completely and utterly alone. The only one who will see me is you.'

For a moment she had him, his dark eyes molten, his fingers moving over her skin, exploring, brushing a nipple so that she mewed with pleasure, arching her back to press further into his hand.

'Raoul,' she whispered. 'Make love to me.'

He spun away so suddenly she was left reeling with his absence. 'I have to go,' he said, his chest rising and falling like a bellow. 'Take your time. I will send Marco later on to fetch the basket.'

And then he was gone. When she recovered enough to look around, she saw his long legs eating up the stone steps three at a time until he reached the top. She watched him stride towards the castle, and she collapsed on the sand, lacking even the energy to rebutton her bodice, feeling as stung and sick as if he'd physically slapped her.

What was happening to her? She was barely married twenty-four hours and her husband was rejecting her, refusing to make love to her when he had already shown how good they could be together.

So what the hell was his problem?

CHAPTER NINE

By the time she returned to the castle, Raoul was gone. 'To the village,' Natania told her, looking sullen again.

'Did he say when he would be back?'

She shook her head and passed her a cup of hot, sweet tea; Gabriella gave up. Natania could not help. How could anybody help when she did not know what the problem was herself?

So she sat in the library to await his return. Maybe Phillipa had been right, after all. Maybe she had rushed into this marriage without talking through the details of each other's expectations. Maybe she should have waited. But it was not too late; they had only been married one day. She flatly refused to believe it was too late. He loved her, she was sure. Otherwise why would he have married her?

So she would wait, and when he returned they would talk.

She busied herself with studying the books in his collection, trying desperately to be interested and get absorbed when she found a rare or first edition, but her heart wasn't in it. Her ears were permanently pricked, waiting for any sound that might signal Raoul's return.

Natania eventually came and brought her a bowl of chunky soup filled with vegetables, crusty bread and local butter; it smelled wonderful but Gabriella could not stomach it and sent it back barely touched.

And, as day slipped into evening, Gabriella knew he intended not to return while she was awake, so she pressed Natania to take her to Raoul's room. 'Are you sure?' the woman asked.

'I have to,' she said. Natania nodded and showed her to his room, not on the first floor as she had expected, but a modest room tucked away behind the kitchen, barely better than servants' quarters.

'He sleeps here?'

Natania nodded. 'Ever since we have worked for him. He will not sleep on the floor above.' She fetched Gabriella a robe and laid it on the bed. 'I am sorry. Even I did not think he could be this cruel or I would have not have let you marry him.'

'I love him,' she said, feeling weak, stupid and totally shell-shocked. 'Nothing could have stopped me marrying him.'

The gypsy woman nodded, her eyes sad. 'I know.'

He watched her sleep, her chestnut hair splayed across his pillow. He physically ached to join her, but he knew he could not. Not if he was ever to let her go.

And he must let her go. She was too precious, too beautiful. She deserved far more than he could ever give her. She deserved better. She deserved a man who might save her if she ever fell...

And yet here she was in his bed, curled up like a kitten, and here he was, rock hard with wanting her. He could take her right now. He could climb into bed, kiss her into wakefulness, caress her sweet curves and bury himself deep in her sweet depths.

He ground his teeth in frustration and growled low in his throat, forcing his feet to stay right where they were.

Why didn't she give up? How many times did he have to reject her before she hated him enough to leave him alone?

He had never taken her for such a fighter.

And he had never taken himself for such a fool. He knew he was capable of being a fool; God, he'd more than proved that eleven years ago, marrying a woman at the end of her career who had wanted the safety blanket of a marriage, while refusing to be satisfied with being out of the limelight, still lusting after the adoration of everyone. The adoration of just one man had not been enough.

He thought he'd learned his lesson then.

But no. He had been a fool to agree to this. He had known it would come unstuck. He had known it could not work. There were other ways to get revenge against a family he hated with his soul without holding someone so precious and innocent hostage in the process.

It was so wrong to hold her hostage.

But he could not afford let her go yet. If he did, she would flee straight into the arms of Garbas and this would all have been for nothing; Umberto's plans would backfire in spectacular fashion. He had not come this far to let a Garbas win now. So he needed to keep her here just a little while longer, just until Garbas was put away for good, and then he would let her go. There had to be someone decent out there for her—someone worthy of her love.

And in the meantime there would be no more picnics on the beach. No more occasions where they could be alone together, even if it meant no more smiles, no more laughter to add to his bank of memories. And, given what he was doing, the last thing he deserved were smiles and laughter.

'I'm sorry, Bella,' he whispered, aching for her, aching for what he had lost before he had ever known the full extent of her love. 'So very sorry.' And he left her sleeping and walked away.

'We need to talk.' It was after lunch and he'd been avoiding her all day, taking his meals alone and forcing her to do likewise, but finally she had managed to track him down to the library.

'Bella,' he said, rising to his feet to greet her with a kiss to her cheeks. 'How lovely to see you. Did you sleep well?'

'Forget it, Raoul. I'm not in the mood.' She didn't want empty platitudes. All morning a storm had been building outside, thick, dark clouds building on the horizon, sweeping in from the sea until they formed a heavy dark bank. All morning a storm had been building inside her, dark and brooding and increasing in intensity.

'Is something wrong?'

'You know it is. I want to know what's going on.'

'I'm afraid you have me at a disadvantage.'

'I don't think so. I think I'm the one at a disadvantage. I gave up on waiting for you to come to my bed, given that was apparently too onerous a task the night we were married, so I slept in your bed last night, hoping you would join me some time through the night.'

'Bella, I am so sorry. I was held up…'

'Doing what? I want to make love with my husband. What is wrong with that?'

'You don't know what you're saying.'

'I do! I just don't understand what you're saying or why you're saying it. I'm your wife, Raoul, and I am going mad here wondering what is wrong with me that you are so interested in doing something else—anything else! But there is nothing wrong with me, so it must be with you. You hide yourself away from me every night; I won't let you do that again. Because I love you, and I want to make love to you. I want you in my bed. I want to be in yours. Why won't you make love to me, now that we are married, when you found no such barrier before? Or is there something painfully wrong with me you haven't told me about?'

'There is nothing wrong with you.'

'Then what the hell is wrong with you? We are married, Raoul. You took me for your wife. What is it you intend to do with me that you bring me to this godforsaken end of the earth and as good as hang me out to dry? What's with that? This is supposed to be our honeymoon.'

He stiffened. 'I did not realise you were so inconvenienced by being here.'

'Inconvenienced? How ungrateful of me to imply such a thing, when clearly I'm having the time of my life! And when I try to seduce you—my own husband—you reject me. You turn me down. How do you think that makes me feel?'

'Gabriella…'

'Do you know how humiliating it is for everyone to know that your own husband will not make love to you?'

'Nobody knows.'

'Except for Natania and Marco. Or is that why you brought me here? To save me the humiliation and indignity of the entire world knowing? Should I thank you instead for your kind consideration?'

'Gabriella, it's not like that.'

'Isn't it? You know, I used to think you had bricked up your heart behind walls so high and thick that they could never be breached. But I thought there was hope for you when we spent those days in Venice. I thought there was hope when you asked me to marry you. But I was wrong.

'Because you don't have a heart at all. You're empty inside. You're not a man, you're a shell. An empty, hollow shell of a man. Devoid of emotion. Devoid of feeling. And I wish to God I'd never met you.'

His jaw was set tight, the cords in his neck pulled taut, and when the words came they sounded like they were ground out. 'You have no idea what I feel.'

'No, I don't. Because you won't tell me. You won't share the slightest thing with me. Me, the woman who is supposed to be your wife! And yet you give me nothing. When I tell you that I love you, I get nothing in return. I don't even know if you love me. I thought you did. I believed you when once you told me that you do not have to hear the words to be true, but now I need to hear those words. Can you say them? Do you love me, Raoul?'

'Bella…'

'Don't *Bella* me! Don't pretend I mean something to you when clearly I mean nothing. Do you love me? It's a simple enough question. Yes or no, Raoul; what's it to be?'

He spun around, his hand raking through his hair. 'Why are you doing this?'

'Because I need to know. I need to hear those words. I need you to prove that they are true.'

His hand slammed down hard on his desk. 'Do you think I wanted this?'

'What are you talking about? You're the one who asked me to marry you. Who insisted on not waiting? Who told me that I was the one who made him want to break his vow never to marry again? You're the one who asked *me* to marry *you*!'

He shook his head wildly from side to side, like a stallion readying for a fight. 'Do you think I wanted a wife who needed a man to love her and cherish her? Do you think I *needed* another wife?'

Thunder rolled overhead, a long, booming sound that filled the silence in the room and turned it toxic.

'But you asked me…' She heard a sob, recognised it as her own and knew she had to escape, knew she had to get as far away as she possibly could from him. She turned and fled out of the room and across the stone entrance-hall, her shoes slapping on the stones.

'Gabriella!' she heard, but she didn't stop. Couldn't

stop. She had to get away, as far away as she could. She tore through the kitchen, looking for escape, finding it in the doors leading to the terrace and the path to the cove, thinking she could hide there, amongst the boulders on the beach, and find the time to work out what she should do.

She would have to leave. She would have to run away, her tail between her legs. Humiliated. Defeated. Phillipa would take her in—Philippa, who had warned her to take her time.

Two short days ago she had been so happy. So wondrously happy. So sure that he loved her.

Do you think I needed another wife?

Hadn't he wanted to marry her? Then why had he asked her? What had she been thinking? Tears streamed down her face, blurring her vision. The bank of dark clouds blotted out the sun, the loose edges like thick, black fingers rolling dark dough across the sky; they rumbled and grumbled with discontent. But still she ran on, faster, towards the stone steps that led down to the beach.

Behind her, she heard him call her name again and ran faster, her grief pushing her on. She flung herself down the time-worn steps to the beach, her feet barely touching the stones, before launching herself onto the sand. The skirt of her dress flew around her; she kicked her flat shoes from her feet at the first opportunity to give her purchase on the sand.

'Gabriella!'

Above her the sky darkened, the waves crashed against the cliff. She heard his voice on the wind that whipped through her hair, filled with salt and moisture from the sea, but she didn't look back. She dared not. There was no point. What was the point of looking back at a man you loved—a man you *thought* you loved—who seemed incapable of loving you but had married you nonetheless?

She could not bear to see him.

Why had he done this to her?

Why?

Her feet pushed on, fighting the loose, soft sand, searching for somewhere to hide, somewhere she could be safe in her misery and despair.

But the sand had been eaten up on the incoming tide and there was nowhere to run. The tide lapped at her feet and she turned back only to collide with a rock that should not have been there. Except this rock was warm, had a thumping heart and had arms that clamped tightly around her.

Raoul.

She looked up at him, panting, desperate and afraid. She saw her storm reflected in his eyes, wild, insane and wanting, as above them the storm broke in a thunderclap that shook the ground and sent the vibrations spiralling through her. They fell on each other like that storm, hungry, wild and insatiable.

Their mouths meshed, their tongues dancing, duelling, her cheek scraping hard against his blue-black beard as she pulled his clothes free with busy, seeking hands, needing to touch him, to feel him; needing to feel his hot flesh against her own.

Rain pelted down upon them, fat droplets that tugged

on their hair, their clothes and stuck the fabric to them, but his hands were hot and liberating; the wet fabric was no barrier to those seeking hands. He groaned in her mouth and spun her away, finding their own private grotto, where he pressed her hard against the stone, and pressed himself hard against her, making her gasp with his size and his need while her own need spiralled out of control. Her hands explored him, fingernails raking his back, relishing the firm, hard flesh, the muscled tone; her fingers traced the lines of his ribs, the nub of his nipples, the thick column of his erection.

He made a sound like a hungry beast, half-growl, half-roar, and she felt her dress tear apart, felt the rain on her hot skin and his hotter hands at her breasts. Felt her bones dissolve as he dropped his hot mouth to one breast, sucking her nipple in tight until she thought she would explode with the agony and the ecstacy, while his large hands travelled her body, heading south, taking away her last remaining scrap of cover.

She battled with his waistband and, still locked together with her at the mouth, he pushed her hands aside and did the job himself; she felt him hard and hot and bucking against her belly.

She felt herself lifted, pressed hard against the smooth stone, her body pulsing as her legs encircled him, throbbing with need, anticipating completion.

Thunder boomed again and lightning rent the sky. She caught sight of his face, wretched, desperate and tortured, and she pulled his face to hers and kissed him so deeply, she knew he must feel her very soul.

She was lost to the storm going on around her, the

storm going on inside, the fury building with the need until he lowered her slowly down.

She felt his hardness in a nudging press, her muscles working to pull him in; her body ached for completion. And yet he held her there, suspended, for what seemed like for ever as his tongue drove into her mouth, demanding every part of her for his own. Until he let her fall as he pressed inside, her mind blew apart in a raging storm of stars.

Nothing could ever be better than this.

The fleeting thought came to her in that one moment of clarity when the world and everything in it was suspended and there existed just this one, intense moment.

Then he moved inside her and her world threatened to come apart. He was so large she felt that she could not let him go without feeling the suck of his organ on her womb, without feeling the need to have him back inside.

She was already on the brink. He thrust again and she gasped with the spiralling sensations shuddering around him, and with the next he cried out and buried himself so deep inside her she wondered if he could ever find his way out.

Her orgasm came in a rolling wave, like the dark clouds had done this day, building and intensifying until there was no way to go but be lost in the thunderclap of her release as she felt him lose himself inside her.

He carried her to the castle wrapped in the shredded remnants of her dress and his damp shirt; he carried her to his bathroom where they soaped each other in the steamy shower, exploring each other's bodies, taking the time they had not had before.

And then he laid her reverently on his bed and acquainted his mouth with every part of her, tasting her, suckling her until she once again cried out, begging for release.

Afterwards he held her close. 'I love you,' she said, and he stilled and kissed her cheek.

'Go to sleep,' he said, holding her close, his voice a husky promise.

She snuggled closer. For she knew in her heart that he loved her, even though he still could not bring himself to say the words for whatever reason he must love her.

She knew it.

Until she woke in the morning to find him gone.

There was a letter on his pillow, barely a note, just two short lines:

I'm sorry.
Please forgive me.

And the bottom dropped out of her world.

CHAPTER TEN

HE HAD gone. Some time this morning before light, according to Natania who had heard the car, he had left her.

Why?

'I thought he loved me,' she said, sitting in Natania's kitchen, sipping sweet tea.

'I told you this was a bad place. You should leave.'

Nothing had ever sounded so tempting. But where to go? Back to Paris, and the big empty house? Or Venice, where she would not be welcome if Raoul was there? 'I don't know where to go.'

'You have a friend in London. Marco can take you to the airport.'

She bit her lip, thinking through the options. Wondering how Phillipa's husband would take the news of her separation so soon after dragging his wife and young baby to Venice for the wedding. 'I don't know. I have to call her, see if it's okay.'

'Call her, then. Or email. There is a computer in the library.'

'You're right. I'll book a ticket while I'm at it. Thank you, Natania. I'm sorry that we could not have met in better circumstances.'

The gypsy woman shook her head, setting the hoops at her ears dancing. 'It is not your fault. I thought you were the one.' She sent her gaze in a wide arc. 'But it is this place. It is what it does to Raoul. It is what it reminds him of. It is a bad place.'

It was a toxic place as far as Gabriella was concerned. It got worse when she realised the computer was password-protected and she couldn't even access her email account, let alone book a flight.

'Damn you, Raoul,' she snarled as she stared at the blinking cursor. On a hunch, she typed 'Raoul'. No luck.

'Raoul Del Arco' met with the same 'invalid password' response.

Out of frustration she typed in 'bastard', half-expecting that one would work—but then, she rationalised when it didn't, anyone could have guessed that; it was hardly secure.

She scanned the desk, looking for somewhere he might have jotted down the password, but the desk was irritatingly paper free. She pulled open a drawer, searching through the papers for something, anything, on which he might have written it down. But she could find nothing and slammed it shut.

The drawer on the other side got similar treatment. This one was almost empty though; mostly stationery supplies. A few pens. A stapler. A key.

That drawer got slammed shut too.

Damn!

Unless, she thought a moment later, there was a filing cabinet somewhere. She opened the drawer again, picked up the key, which was heavy, despite its small

size, and ornately carved. Maybe it was not like any fil-
ing-cabinet key she had ever seen before, but then this
was Raoul and his filing cabinet was no doubt antique.

She prowled the library, testing any piece of furniture
with a lock, but most were already unlocked and the key
did not fit. She studied it in the palm of her hand. Why
keep a key that fitted no lock?

Then she remembered the door at the end of the passageway.

The locked door. And she wondered…

What had he done? Raoul drove aimlessly through village after village of simple white stone buildings and
small fields set amidst the rocky hills, knowing only
that he needed to get away—except there was no getting away from his own black thoughts.

For he had done the unthinkable. He had done what
he had promised himself he would not do. He was supposed to keep her safe; he was supposed to protect her.

Instead he had given in to his basest self. He had
taken advantage of her sweet body, and he had not been
able to stop at just once.

And it didn't matter that she had provoked him, that
she had goaded him with her taunts and her words.
Nothing mattered except that he was in the wrong,
whichever way he looked at it. He had been in the wrong
from the very beginning.

He had set out to marry her, to do anything it took to
keep her and Garbas apart, and he had done that. But in
the process he had lost Gabriella.

You don't have to love her.

The old man's words came back to him. He'd taken the words at face value. They had seemed cold but they had made sense. And he had intended to keep himself apart. He would not love her; he could not afford to, not if he was to set her free.

He hadn't meant to love her.

He pulled the car to a halt near a *horreo*, a corn shed that looked like a miniature stone cathedral, his palms sweating on the wheel.

He hadn't meant to love her.

But he did.

He looked at the *horreo*, reminded of the stone castle where he had brought her and then abandoned her. What would she be thinking? How would she be feeling? After giving her the cold shoulder since their wedding, they had shared a night of exquisite pleasure—he had lost count of how many times they had made love—and then he had cold-heartedly walked away.

His hands were sweaty on the steering wheel.

Their love-making had been so frantic and desperate that he had not even thought to use protection.

Even now she could be carrying his child.

What had he done?

He had run from the truth. He had not even been able to bring himself to tell her he loved her. Surely she deserved at least that?

But then, she deserved so much more. She deserved an explanation. She deserved his apology. After which she probably would not want his love.

But he had to tell her.

He put the car into gear and turned it around on the

narrow road, only then noticing the dark bank of cloud that extended along the coast. And with a sizzle of apprehension he was reminded of another time, another day long ago, when the cloud gathered heavy over the castle and he had been rushing to get back.

Only to have his world crash and burn when he had.

He wasn't superstitious; he didn't believe in Natania's gypsy folklore that she would spout whenever she got the chance. But, still, there was a bad feeling in the pit of his stomach and he put his foot down.

She slipped the key into the lock where it fitted like a hand in a glove and held her breath, turning it with a solid click. She looked around, wondering if anyone had heard her. But Natania was busy in the kitchen and Marco was with her. Besides, the way the wind outside was building, nobody would possibly hear.

She turned the knob, easing it around, her heart hammering in her chest as she pushed open the door. It was dark, soft, grey light filtering in through a grimy window, dust motes playing in the shifting air. She found a switch and flicked it to and fro but nothing happened. And then she could see enough in the dim light to make out a dresser, an oil lamp on top, a stack of boxes in one corner and a circular staircase rising up on the other side of the room.

Everything was musty. The dust tickled her nose and she thought about leaving. Some kind of store room, he had said, and she could believe him. Clearly she had imagined it when she had thought she had seen someone entering.

But why would Raoul keep it locked and why would he secrete the key in his desk downstairs?

Something banged upstairs and she jumped. Then it banged again. A shutter come loose in the wind, she guessed.

The staircase beckoned. Maybe the answers were upstairs, in the turret room itself. She found matches by the lamp, lifted the glass and held a match to the wick, hissing and spluttering, filling the glass and the room with soft white light. Then, holding it carefully, she started to climb the creaky stairs.

Outside the wind started to howl, a sound that conspired with the banging to make a home in the back of her neck, prickling as if someone unseen had run their finger along her skin.

She shivered. *Next she'd be seeing ghosts.* Warily, tentatively, she peered through the hole at the top of the stairs, the doorway to the turret room. It was dark but for the shutter slamming repeatedly against the wall letting in a thready glow of grey light. She stepped up into the room, holding out the lamp as she circled, stunned beyond measure.

It was someone's idea of a fantasy bedroom, something from *The Arabian Nights* or similar. The bed was low and covered in rich red silks and brightly coloured cushions with gold trim and tassels, dusty now, but still a glorious splash of colour. The walls were hung with jewel-coloured silk wall-hangings and covered in portraits: a ballerina, stunningly beautiful, photographed in costume in every ballet imaginable, *Swan Lake, Giselle, Romeo and Juliet.*

And there on the dresser was a close-up of her laughing into the camera, beautiful, glamorous and so full of life. Gabriella put down the lamp and picked up the picture in her hands.

To Raoul, she had written in large, elegant letters. *All my love, Katia.*

Katia. *Raoul's first wife.*

A chill went down her spine. This was Katia's room, kept as it must have been when she was alive. Kept locked and preserved, like some kind of shrine.

Was that why he hadn't wanted another wife? Was that why they had come here, to be close to his first wife. Because he was still in love with Katia?

Pain lanced her heart. She'd thought she had sensed something holding him in reserve. It had not been there when he had made love to her; he had loved her then.

Or so she had thought.

Raoul drove the last few kilometres with a growing sense of dread. It wasn't the approaching storm, but the fear that Gabriella had already left. What had she to stay for, after all? He had left her. There was nothing for her here.

But as he neared the castle something else caught his attention and froze his blood solid. There was a light on that shouldn't be there, a flickering light in the turret room—*just as there had been that day all those years ago.*

And suddenly he wasn't afraid that she had already left.

He was afraid that she had stayed…

* * *

The wind howled around the windows, cold fingers searching for a way in, the shutter banging endlessly, threatening to shatter what was left of her already bruised and battered nerves. She put the picture down and crossed to the window, testing the latch. It was stuck, probably grown shut through years of disuse.

Down below she could hear the surf smashing against the cliff, sending spray raining skywards. The window budged, little by little. If she just pushed a little harder, it would come unstuck.

He took the stairs three at a time, bellowing for Marco and Natania, wishing Gabriella would stick her head out of a door and demand to know what was wrong, fearing all the time that she would not—that he was already too late.

He reached the landing and turned right, standing panting and gutted when he saw it—the door to the turret room open, the flickering light from the lamp dancing down the stairs.

'Gabriella!' he shouted, leaping onto the stairs. 'Gabriella, where are you?'

She pushed against the glass with all her weight just as the clap of thunder burst from the skies, but it was the feeling that someone had just called her name that had her looking over her shoulder at the same moment the window finally gave. She didn't have time to see if there was anyone there; the wind clamped icy fingers around the open window and flung it open, dragging her from her feet. She screamed, clinging to the catch, her legs battling for purchase on the window sill while the surf boiled and spewed on the rocks below.

'Nooo!' he roared, feeling the past come crashing back, dark and horrific.

This could not be happening again!

He flew across the room, red spots before his eyes, the colour of blood in the white sea foam. He caught hold of her leg and then her waist. 'Let go!' he yelled at her. Her fingers were still wound deathly tight around the window clasp.

Finally she seemed to realise he had her and let go. He spun her inside, into his arms and against his frantically beating heart, stroking her hair with one hand, keeping the other wound tightly around her while the wind swirled and screamed into the room. 'What the hell were you doing?'

'The shutter was banging.'

'No,' he said, relief giving way to anger. 'What the hell were you doing in here?'

She pushed him away, ran her hands through her hair as if she was fine, but she was trembling and as white as a ghost, her chest rising and falling quickly as she tried to catch her breath. 'I was looking for a password for your computer so I could book a flight out of here. I found a key instead.'

'And you thought you'd go exploring?' Behind them the shutter and the window both slammed, rain slanting inside, feeling like icy needles against their skin. He growled and yanked the shutter closed before securing the window.

'You told me it was a store room.'

'It is.'

The storm let loose outside, the thunder overhead,

lightning piercing the gloom and letting loose a fresh burst of rain against the shutters. 'You didn't tell me what it stored. You didn't tell me you kept it as a shrine to the woman you love.'

'Is that what you think?'

'What else could it be? No wonder you said you never wanted another wife. You already had one—all her photographs, all her mementos, locked away safe and sound for whenever you wanted to spend a moment or two with her. I never believed you slept downstairs near the kitchen. This is where you spent the first two nights of our marriage, isn't it? Tucked away with the memories of a dead woman!'

And he cursed himself for thinking he could lock away his past behind a closed door and keep it there for ever. 'You have no idea how wrong you are.'

'Am I? You brought me here because you couldn't bear to be apart from her. You married me, but once we were here you had no use for me. Because there was no room for me in our marriage, not when you had her.'

'No!'

'Because you are still in love with her!'

'No! That's where you are wrong. If this room was kept as a shrine, it was as a shrine to my own stupidity—a reminder of how naive a man can be when he believes in love.

'I stopped loving Katia a long time ago when I discovered my love was worth nothing. When she used this room to betray me!'

She looked around uncertainly. 'Katia...?'

'She brought her lovers here. Her little secret room,

her *love nest*, complete with an escape route in case someone came looking. In case I called for her.'

She shook her head, holding her arms around her waist, her hair stuck down around her face. 'I didn't see any escape—'

'There is a railing outside the window—or there was—and footholds in the rock. Easy enough when the weather was fine, perilous when it was not. But she didn't seem to care. It was a game she played, you see, a risky, dangerous game—trying to outsmart me, and succeeding. Until that storm-ridden night.'

She swallowed, remembering the surging sea, angry and frothing below the castle like a wild animal snapping and snarling to be fed, and felt a chill run down her spine. She could not imagine trying to be out there with just a railing and footholds between her and the violent sea. 'Katia died here, didn't she? She and her lover fell to their deaths.'

'Now do you understand why I keep that door locked?'

He turned away, closing his eyes to blot out those images, his hands fisting in his hair. But he could still picture the scene just as clearly as if it had happened yesterday—Manuel, already disappearing from view as Raoul had run up the last few stairs into the room, roaring and almost frothing at the mouth in his fury and rage; Katia urging Manuel to hurry, as she herself had taken one look at Raoul, her eyes bright with the thrill of the game, her hair whipping around her face and her laughter still ringing out in his mind.

He had been so angry and filled with rage, rage that

filled the black empty hole from where his heart had been ripped; he had been paralysed with shock. His feet had been stuck to the floor while his world, his dreams and his love had disintegrated around him.

For she had betrayed him.

She had laughed at him.

And, even when he had heard the grating, tearing sound of metal from rock, even when he had heard Manuel's cry as he had fallen from the broken railing— even when he had heard Katia's desperate cry as she had realised the game was no longer fun—he had stood there a moment too long, transfixed, broken and shattered, wondering what the hell had gone wrong.

A moment of inaction he would pay for for his entire life.

He reeled away from the window. What use was a pathetic lock? He should have bricked up the door to this poisoned room and its sordid memories years ago.

He felt her hand on his shoulder. 'Raoul...'

'Don't,' he said. 'You would not want to touch me if you knew.'

'If I knew what?'

'The truth. I came back to tell you. I could not leave you like I had, not without you knowing everything.'

Spiders crawled up her back; the light from the lamp flickered ominously. 'What do you mean?'

'I mean the truth about why I married you.'

CHAPTER ELEVEN

THE air in the turret room was too thin to breathe, the raging storm outside a soundtrack for what was going on in her head. Here, in this room, her future lay in the balance. He had come back. He had left her this morning but he had come back, as she had wanted him to, as she had prayed. Except now she wasn't sure she wanted to hear what he had to say.

'So why did you marry me?'

'Gabriella—Bella—I have so much for which to seek your forgiveness.'

'No, forget about forgiveness. Tell me why you married me. Clearly it was not, as I imagined in my pathetic little brain, because you loved me.'

'I… It shames me to say that it was not.'

She squeezed her eyes shut and sagged into a chair, uncaring about the dust that welled up in a cloud. Right now she had more important things on her mind, like the heart that lay trampled and bleeding all over the floor. 'Then tell me why.'

'I made a promise. To a man I loved and respected above all others. A man who had been like a father to me. Even though I knew it was wrong, even though I knew I could not be the husband you needed, I made that promise to him.'

She looked up at him, chilled to the bone, knowing there could be only one man who would have made him promise such a thing. 'My grandfather made you promise to marry me?'

'He was dying, Bella. He was worried about you.'

She remembered the visit he'd made before Umberto's death, the conversation he'd skirted around when she'd asked him for the details. But it was too impossible to believe, too horrendous; hysteria built inside her like magma ready to erupt at any moment. 'You promised to marry me because my grandfather asked you to?'

'He wanted to be sure you would be safe when he was gone.'

She put the heels of her hand to her forehead, the drumming in her temples growing louder, the pressure growing heavy and insistent behind her brow. It was insane. Did he actually realise what he was saying?

Suddenly she couldn't sit. She sprang to her feet, pacing the floor. 'And you agreed to this? You said, *anything you ask, Umberto; of course I will marry her?*'

'I tried to tell him—'

'You told him you would marry me—so you lured me into a loveless marriage only to dump me in a godforsaken castle in Spain where your dead wife rides shotgun—'

'*No!* I told him it wouldn't work. I told him I would make no kind of husband. I told him you would hardly be safe with me—a man who had not been able to save his own wife. How could you be safe with me?'

'And yet you still said yes. You took me to Venice and you set out to seduce me. You made love to me! I thought you loved me, Raoul. When you held me in your arms and you made love to me, I thought you *loved* me! But you lied, every one of those times you kissed me. Every one of those times we lay in bed together, every one of them was a lie!'

He took a step closer and held out one hand to her. 'No, Bella.'

She turned away. She never wanted to touch him again. 'And all the time you couldn't wait to be rid of me. You couldn't wait to drop the pretence and dump me.'

'It wasn't like that.'

She spun back around. 'You deceived me!'

'What choice did I have? Marry you, or say no to Umberto and watch Garbas get his greedy hooks in you?'

She stilled, her breathing hard and frantic in her chest, her mind seizing on the one thing that finally pulled the pieces together. 'This is all about Consuelo? Grandfather was so worried about my friendship with him that he would get his henchman to marry me? Why couldn't he have just warned me if he was so worried?'

'Would you have listened—you, who always sees the best in everyone? You, who could not believe he was a criminal even when he was charged with fraud by the police? Try to see it from Umberto's point of view: Garbas knew you would inherit as soon as you turned twenty-five. Umberto wanted to ensure you would be safe from his greed.'

She shook her head. 'Even if what you say is true,

what danger is Consuelo to me now that he's been charged?' And even as she said the words a creeping suspicion filtered into her psyche, no more than a floating piece of black silk on the wind at first, it took shape and form and became three-dimensional and ugly.

'You were responsible for that, weren't you. It was no surprise to you that day of the funeral—no surprise that Consuelo had disappeared. Because you already knew. You were the one who tipped off the authorities. You— you wanted to be sure he could not touch me. You got Consuelo arrested.'

'He's a criminal, Bella. It's no more than he deserves.'

She blinked, appalled at his implied confession, horrified by the sheer magnitude of his machinations—all to ensure she would marry him. 'You don't even try to deny it. You always hated Consuelo. Always!'

'And why wouldn't I hate him? He was the one who called me asking for money one too many times and, when I refused and told him he was a fool, he gloated that I was the fool and that his brother was having an affair with my wife! He gloated that I was the last to know, that everyone—*everyone*—knew and were laughing about me behind my back.'

A bolt of lightning squeezed through the shutters; a blast of thunder rent the skies and rumbled long into the distance.

'Consuelo's brother died here...' she said.

'Manuel was having an affair with my wife. He was supposed to be a friend. They were *both* supposed to be my friends.'

'And you were so worried I would marry someone

who did the dirty on you that you put me through all this. How considerate of you.'

'He's a scumbag, Bella. You deserve better.'

'*He's* a scumbag?' She looked up at him, wondering how she could ever have imagined that she loved him—someone who manipulated people, facts and the truth to gain his own ends. 'So what the hell does that make you?'

She saw him flinch. She was glad that she could cause him half the pain he had caused her. 'The joke's on you, of course,' she continued. 'For I had no intention of marrying Consuelo. Yes, I liked him—but as a friend, that was all. Maybe you might have given me some credit for making my own decisions.'

'You think he would have left you alone, knowing you were coming into your inheritance? Don't kid yourself. It was the money he was interested in.'

'Maybe you're right. It would not be the first time I had fallen prey to a man who wanted nothing more but to use me and abuse me for his own purposes.'

'Bella, listen to me…'

'Why should I, when all you have ever told me is lies?'

'No. Hear me out. Yes, what I did was wrong, but I was bound by a promise I had made to a dying man. I would marry you, I had decided, but I was going to let you go—once I knew you were safe. I wanted you to find someone worthy of you, who loved you for who you were and not how much money you had.'

'How very noble of you. And meanwhile you lock me up in some cold, barren castle in Spain and pretend you are not interested in me. Or were you pretending when we did make love?'

'That was never a pretence.'

She nodded but she could not bring herself to look at him. 'Maybe. But your love was. That's where I have an issue. Our marriage is a sham, Raoul, a complete and utter sham. I want a divorce as soon as it can be arranged.'

'Bella—Gabriella—please, give me a chance to explain. I left today because I was disgusted with myself. I had promised myself I would protect you. I would keep you safe, and when it was safe I would let you go where you could find the love of a good man—a worthy man. I would not stop you.

'Except I did not realise I was already falling in love with you. I thought that, if I didn't say it, it wouldn't matter, that it wouldn't count. But last night, when we made love in the storm, and afterwards in my bed, I could not deny what had already happened to me in Venice. And today, instead of fleeing, I had to turn around to tell you. I love you, Gabriella. I had to come back and ask for your forgiveness and to tell you I love you with my life.'

She laughed. Insanely. Manically. Whether it was a delayed reaction to the shock of almost falling from the window onto the rocks below, or a reaction to the callous way he had treated her, she didn't know. But the sound was cathartic, strengthening her, increasing her resolve. 'And now, when everything else has come unstuck, you serve up with the one thing you know I have been waiting for. The one thing I have been begging for you to say all along.'

'Bella, it's not like that.'

'Isn't it? Isn't this the last card you have to play, the final roll of the die? Your last feeble attempt to keep me prisoner in a loveless marriage? But it won't work, Raoul. Not now. Because I don't believe you. And, even if I did, it doesn't matter any more because I don't want your love. Not if this is the way you show it.'

'Gabriella...'

'No,' she said, standing strong now with a new resolve. She'd been a fool but she had survived, and she would keep on surviving all by herself. 'I don't want to know. Just arrange that divorce, Raoul. I want to be free of you and I want it now.'

CHAPTER TWELVE

MARCO told him she was there, waiting for him at the sea door—with the signed papers, no doubt, though why she hadn't sent them via her lawyer he had no idea. Maybe she thought she had left something here.

He was on his way down to her when he spotted it, the paperweight sitting on his desk, the paperweight she had bought for him that day in Murano. He lifted it up to the light, watched the way its dark layers spun and floated around the blood-red core, the darkness lightening as the layers rose until they faded into the clear glass. He shook his head.

Even Gabriella, who had always seen the good in people, would not make the mistake of selecting such a thing for him again.

He remembered the way she had presented it to him, intending it to be a parting gift, except he had not been able to let her go. Not then.

Except he had not realised why.

What a fool he had been.

He sighed, replacing it on his desk. It was all he had of her now, and even that was more than he deserved.

She was waiting in the gondola, looking more beautiful than he had ever seen her, a soft pastel dress showing off her long, tan legs, her hair braided around her face, falling free around her bare shoulders. Just looking at her was enough to slice his broken heart anew.

'Gabriella,' he said, relishing the taste of her name on his lips. 'Would you not come inside?'

She smiled a little, or maybe she just pressed her lips together, and shook her head. 'I thought we might meet on neutral ground. Or, in this case, neutral territory at least.' This time she did smile and he noticed for the first time the strain lines around her eyes, the tightness in her features, as though she was battling to keep herself in control. 'Will you join me?'

She could have asked him to fly to the moon with her and he would have said yes. As he climbed aboard, he noticed the folio tucked by her side. 'You brought the papers?'

'I brought them.'

And something inside him died, something unreasonable—because it was unreasonable to hope that she had changed her mind after all he had put her through, even if he wished it could be so. He had spent two months in his own personal hell, wishing he had done things differently, wishing he had never agreed to Umberto's deathbed wishes, wishing he had been man enough to follow his gut and refuse.

But he had not refused, and now she had come with the papers that would be the death warrant to their marriage.

'How did you know to find me here?' he asked as the

gondolier gently negotiated the vessel into the wider canals, and she smiled again, easier this time.

'Lucky guess. I figured that not even you would want
to stay in that mausoleum of a castle a moment longer
than you had to.'

Even he had to smile at that. 'It is good to see you,
Bella.'

She blinked up at him. 'And you.'

'You could have posted the papers.'

'I know, but there were still some things I didn't understand. I have spent two months trying to hate you.
Two months trying to forget. But there are still some
things that will not let me go.' She shook her head. 'I
could not ask those things by mail.'

'What things?'

'Like the ghost story you told me that foggy night we
were here in Venice—the story of the merchant who lost
his wife to two brothers. That was no legend. That was
your story, wasn't it?'

'It was mine.'

She breathed out. 'You made it sound like the merchant had killed them both. But it wasn't like that, was
it?'

'It might as well have been.'

The gondola slipped along the canals, turning this
way and that, the movement of the boat strangely sooth-
ing despite the subject matter.

'So tell me.'

And it was his turn to pause. 'I should have seen it
coming. She was a ballet dancer, as you know, famous
the world over. But she was at the end of her career, and

she craved the adulation of the audience. I should have
known she would never be happy with just one man
when she was used to the adulation of a crowd. Everyone
but me, it seemed, knew about her secret room. I think
in the end she hated me because I didn't know, that I was
foolish enough to believe that she actually loved me.

'And, when I found out it was true, I was in such a
rage, it was no wonder that even in the midst of a storm
they fled from me. I could not have saved Manuel—
the railing was old and rusty and pulled away from the
stone—but Katia…'

He squeezed his eyes shut. 'She cried out and I was so
angry, so tortured, that for a moment I could not move.
And when I did it was too late.'

He felt her hand slide between his and he opened his
eyes in surprise. She smiled sadly. 'How do you know
you would have reached her in time?'

He shook his head. 'That is my curse. I will never
know.'

She gazed up at him. 'That's why you feared you
could not keep me safe, isn't it? You feared you could
not keep anyone safe.'

'How could I keep anyone safe? I could never trust
myself again.'

'But you did save me, Raoul. Don't you remember?
When the wind caught that window and pulled me from
my feet, you were there to stop me falling. You saved
me, Raoul.'

He shook his head. 'I surprised you. I made you turn.
If I hadn't come…'

'I could have fallen. But you saved me.' She nodded

then, taking a deep breath. 'I think I understand now, at least some of it.'

'What do you mean?'

'I mean I've been spending a lot of time thinking these last two months. Remembering. Pulling those weeks apart and trying to work out what happened. And I keep coming back to you trying to walk away. That night in Paris when you put me in a taxi and strode into the rain—you were walking away from Umberto's promise then, weren't you?'

'I didn't want to hurt you. If there was another way to keep you safe, I would do it. But you would not let me.'

'Because I came to your hotel in the morning.'

'You wanted my help to defend Garbas and when I refused you were going to do it all by yourself. I had to get you out of Paris.'

'And so you brought me here to Venice, to seduce me, to convince me to marry you.'

'Bella, I'm not proud of what I did.'

'Maybe it's not so bad, what you did. Or maybe why you did it.'

He turned towards her, trying to find a meaning to her cryptic comment. But she was looking ahead, avoiding his gaze, staring at the buildings now turning softly golden with the lowering sun. 'They called me, you know, several times—Consuelo's lawyers.'

'What did they want?'

'Money. I turned twenty-five last week. Consuelo thought I might like to donate to his defence fund.'

'What did you tell them?'

'That I had better things to do with my money. You were right; he would have sucked me dry.'

She looked at him then. 'I went to the hospital where Consuelo's foundation was based. I went to talk to the director to see what I could do about providing for a new foundation to support those children undergoing chemotherapy, those left in the cold without funding after the collapse of the foundation. He told me that someone had already taken care of it. That someone had already covered what they had lost in the foundation and more.'

She hesitated and looked up him with tears in her eyes. 'That was you, Raoul. You funded the programme, so no child's treatment would be interrupted. So those children's lives might be saved.'

He saw the setting sun in her eyes, saw the golden light dance in her tears. 'I felt responsible.'

Moisture tracked down her cheeks. 'And for two months I have been trying to find a reason to hate you, to believe you had no heart—but everywhere I look, everything I remember, makes the pieces fall another way. And then, with learning of one generous act of kindness, I knew I was wrong. How could I hate a man who did such a thing?'

He smiled, her words a balm to his soul. 'I am glad you don't hate me, Bella. I have lived in hell these past months thinking that.'

She sniffed. 'And so I was wondering…'

He lifted her chin with one hand and rubbed the tears from her cheeks with the thumb of the other; his touch made her catch her breath. 'Tell me,' he said, his voice a husky, deep whisper that carried an urgency that rippled through her bones.

'You once said that you loved me. I threw it back in your face. I thought you were lying. But did you mean it? Was it true, Raoul?'

'That I love you?' He exhaled in a rush. 'Oh, Bella, I know I have betrayed your trust. I know I hurt you so much. And God knows I didn't want to fall in love with you. I didn't think it was possible. But every time we made love, every time I looked at you, I couldn't help but fall in love with you that bit more.

'And it scared me, Bella. I knew you would leave me one day, and I knew it would kill me—so I tried to push you away, but it didn't work.

'Because I do love you, Bella, and I always will. And, if there is ever a way to make up for the way I have treated you, so help me I will track it down, I will pin it to the ground and I will spend my entire life making it up to you.'

'Oh, Raoul.' She put a hand to his cheek, felt the familiar brush of his blue-black beard against her palm, never wanting to have to remember what that felt like again. 'I love you so much, Raoul.'

His mouth found hers and they kissed as the gondola slipped silently beneath the Bridge of Sighs.

'About those papers…' she whispered when finally they had come up for air.

'What about them?'

'Do you think it would hurt if we didn't fill them in? If we gave our marriage another go? With just you and me this time. Nobody else. And no ghosts from the past.'

He smiled at her and her heart flipped over. 'Definitely no ghosts from the past. Just you and me, starting again.' He picked up her hand and kissed it. 'You have made me the happiest man in the world, Bella. You have given me something I thought I would never have, something I thought I had forfeited any right to for ever: you have given me your love. And I will treat it like the treasure it is.'

He dipped his head and kissed her again, so sweet and rich with feeling this time that her head spun and the blood fizzed her veins until she was dizzy on bubbles and the hot taste of him in her mouth.

And that night, in the big bed in the lover's alcove, they solemnly repeated their marriage vows, with the sirens, satyrs, gods and goddesses as their witnesses, smiling this time. Knowing this time it was for real.

* * * * *

COMING NEXT MONTH from Harlequin Presents®
AVAILABLE JANUARY 22, 2013

#3113 SOLD TO THE ENEMY
Sarah Morgan

Leandro Ziakas is her father's most hated business rival, and the only man who can help Selene Antaxos. But within a matter of days she's seduced, bedded and betrayed—and realizes she's sold her soul to the enemy!

#3114 UNCOVERING THE SILVERI SECRET
Melanie Milburne

Heiress Bella Haverton is furious that Edoardo Silveri has been named her guardian. This commanding, enigmatic man has a lethal sex appeal, and time is running out for her to uncover the secrets behind the man who controls her destiny....

#3115 BARTERING HER INNOCENCE
Trish Morey

Luca Barbarigo has waited three long years to exact his revenge against Valentina Henderson. One unforgettable night together left him with nothing but X-rated memories and the sting of her hand across his jaw. But they are the least of her crimes....

#3116 DEALING HER FINAL CARD
Princes Untamed
Jennie Lucas

Her body for a million dollars. With everything to lose, and the weight of Prince Valdimir's gaze upon her, Bree Dalton will have to play the best she's ever played—or run the risk of losing herself completely....

You can find more information on upcoming Harlequin® titles, free excerpts and more at www.Harlequin.com.

EXPHPCNM0113RA

#3117 IN THE HEAT OF THE SPOTLIGHT
The Bryants: Powerful & Proud
Kate Hewitt
Ambitious tycoon Luke Bryant's power and passion will lay scandalous Aurelie bare.... She's determined not to let him get beneath her skin, but faced with the sexiest man she's ever met, Aurelie can't resist just one touch!

#3118 NO MORE SWEET SURRENDER
Scandal in the Spotlight
Caitlin Crews
Ivan Korovin's only solution to a PR nightmare created by outspoken Miranda Sweet is to give the ravenous public what they want—to see these two enemies become lovers! But soon the mutually beneficial charade becomes too hot to handle!

#3119 PRIDE AFTER HER FALL
Lucy Ellis
Lorelai is an heiress on the edge, hiding her desperation behind her glossy blond hair and even brighter smile. Legendary racing driver Nash Blue never could resist a challenge—and he begins his biggest yet: unwrapping the real Lorelai St James....

#3120 LIVING THE CHARADE
Michelle Conder
When buttoned-up Miller Jacob needs to find a fake boyfriend, Valentino Ventura, maverick of the racing world, is the last person she wants. Up for the job, Valentino can't wait to help Miller let her hair—and whatever else she wants—down!

You can find more information on upcoming Harlequin® titles, free excerpts and more at www.Harlequin.com.

EXPHPCNM0113RB

REQUEST YOUR FREE BOOKS!

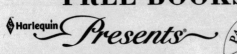 

2 FREE NOVELS PLUS
2 FREE GIFTS!

YES! Please send me 2 FREE Harlequin Presents® novels and my 2 FREE gifts (gifts are worth about $10). After receiving them, if I don't wish to receive any more books, I can return the shipping statement marked "cancel." If I don't cancel, I will receive 6 brand-new novels every month and be billed just $4.30 per book in the U.S. or $4.99 per book in Canada. That's a saving of at least 14% off the cover price! It's quite a bargain! Shipping and handling is just 50¢ per book in the U.S. and 75¢ per book in Canada.* I understand that accepting the 2 free books and gifts places me under no obligation to buy anything. I can always return a shipment and cancel at any time. Even if I never buy another book, the two free books and gifts are mine to keep forever.

106/306 HDN FERQ

Name	(PLEASE PRINT)

Address	Apt. #

City	State/Prov.	Zip/Postal Code

Signature (if under 18, a parent or guardian must sign)

Mail to the **Reader Service:**
IN U.S.A.: P.O. Box 1867, Buffalo, NY 14240-1867
IN CANADA: P.O. Box 609, Fort Erie, Ontario L2A 5X3

Not valid for current subscribers to Harlequin Presents books.

**Are you a current subscriber to Harlequin Presents books
and want to receive the larger-print edition?
Call 1-800-873-8635 or visit www.ReaderService.com.**

* Terms and prices subject to change without notice. Prices do not include applicable taxes. Sales tax applicable in N.Y. Canadian residents will be charged applicable taxes. Offer not valid in Quebec. This offer is limited to one order per household. All orders subject to credit approval. Credit or debit balances in a customer's account(s) may be offset by any other outstanding balance owed by or to the customer. Please allow 4 to 6 weeks for delivery. Offer available while quantities last.

Your Privacy—The Reader Service is committed to protecting your privacy. Our Privacy Policy is available online at www.ReaderService.com or upon request from the Reader Service.

We make a portion of our mailing list available to reputable third parties that offer products we believe may interest you. If you prefer that we not exchange your name with third parties, or if you wish to clarify or modify your communication preferences, please visit us at www.ReaderService.com/consumerschoice or write to us at Reader Service Preference Service, P.O. Box 9062, Buffalo, NY 14269. Include your complete name and address.

HP11B